CLASH OF THE CRYPTIDS

PART 2

A NICOLE BERETTI THRILLER

LUKA T. JACOBS

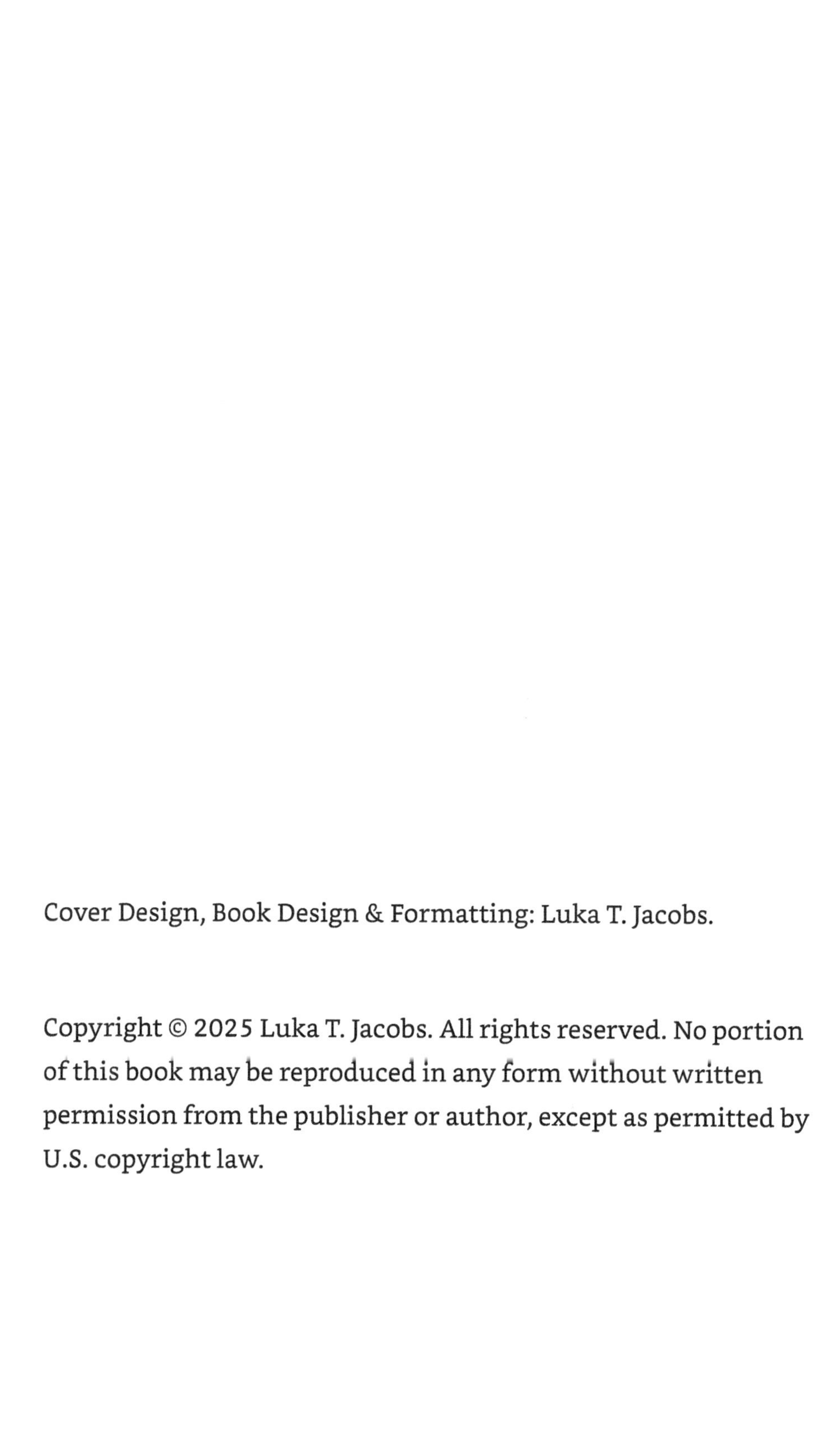

For the readers who keep turning the pages,
this book exists because of you.

FROM THE AUTHOR

Dear Reader,

Thank you for continuing the journey with Part 2 of *Clash of the Cryptids*. Where Part 1 focused on unraveling the past, Part 2 brings the full weight of the storm. The stakes are higher, the dangers more immediate, and Nicole is forced to face everything she's learned in the harshest light possible.

If you haven't read Part One yet, I recommend starting there so the story makes sense.

I hope this conclusion delivers the tension, action and emotional depth you've come to expect.

As always, thank you for being part of this journey.

Happy reading,

Luka T. Jacobs

CONTENTS

PROLOGUE

The town of Blackridge moved through its morning like it always had: quiet, unhurried, and blissfully unaware.

Beretti drove with one hand on the wheel, eyes fixed ahead as the SUV rolled through the heart of town. On the sidewalks, locals bundled in layers strolled with dogs on leashes. A mother adjusted a scarf around her daughter's chin outside the bakery. A teenager zipped by on an e-bike, earphones in his ears.

It looked peaceful. Normal.

But Jacobi knew better. So did Beretti.

They passed the old feed store with the sagging awning, then the rust-red post office. Beretti made a slow right onto Black Crow Lane, and Jacobi noticed something change in her.

Her expression flattened. Shoulders squared. Eyes

narrowed just slightly, like she was staring down a path she didn't want to walk.

He didn't comment. Just watched the quiet shift settle into her posture.

About a mile up, she slowed and turned into a narrow driveway. The house that came into view looked like it had been resting for a very long time.

It was a low-slung, single-story farmhouse with faded white siding and dark gray trim. The lawn surrounding it was surprisingly well-kept, mowed back in a wide circle that reached roughly forty yards in every direction. Beyond that, the grass grew longer, gradually giving way to tree line and bramble at the edges. A few garden beds hugged the front of the house, nothing elaborate, but tidy. The concrete path leading to the porch was swept clean.

Beretti parked and killed the engine.

Jacobi looked toward the house. "Friend or family?"

"Neither," she said. "Old neighbor of mine."

She reached for the door handle, then paused. "Tania cornered me in the bathroom last night at Iron Howl."

Jacobi looked over. "Yeah? What'd she want?"

"She said a lot of things. But one of them was that if I wanted the truth, I should come see Ole Man Richards."

Jacobi frowned. "What does that mean?"

Beretti opened her door. "I guess we're about to find out."

They stepped out as a bird called once from somewhere in the trees, but otherwise the world around them was still.

Beretti knocked twice on the screen door.

It creaked slightly under the weight of her hand.

A moment later, the screen door creaked slightly as the interior door behind it swung open with a long moan from its hinges.

A man stood just inside, seventy, maybe older. Tall but slightly hunched, with a narrow face and sharp eyes set deep beneath thick white brows. His jaw hadn't seen a razor in days, and a wool cardigan hung loosely from his shoulders.

He peered at them without blinking. "What can I do for you folks?"

Beretti straightened. "Mr. Richards? My name is Nicole.

This is FBI Special Agent Jacobi. We're working with the sheriff's office, looking into some unusual predator sightings in the area. Would you mind if we came in for a quick word?"

The old man studied her for a long second. His eyes settled on hers, long enough that Jacobi thought he might close the door without another word.

But finally, Richards stepped back and swung the screen door wider. "Come in. It'd be nice to have some company."

The interior was simple, clean, even comforting. The carpet was a worn mustard color, the furniture a faded brown floral, probably from the early seventies. Everything was in its place. Not a newspaper or mug out of order.

An old television buzzed quietly in the far corner, its color faded and edges curved. On the screen, the cast of *The Golden Girls* shared a laugh. A woman sat in a recliner facing it, motionless except for the slight twitch of one hand. She didn't look their way.

"My wife, Dora," Richards said as he gestured them inside. "She's not ignoring you. Just doesn't really leave that show anymore. Dementia's been gettin' worse this past year. But that program, she still laughs at it."

"I'm sorry to hear that," Jacobi said quietly.

Richards nodded like he'd heard it plenty. "Would you two like some water? Coffee?"

"No, thank you," Beretti said.

He moved with slow, careful steps, settling into the recliner opposite his wife's. He gestured for them to take the couch.

"Apologies. Name's Edwin Richards, though most around here just call me Ole Man Richards. Habit, I guess. Been here long enough."

Jacobi smiled politely. "Appreciate you letting us in, sir."

Richards waved it off. "You're with this pretty lady. You're alright."

Beretti sat forward slightly. "We're tracking a few incidents around the outskirts of town. Animals taken, a couple of attacks. We've been asking around. Thought maybe you'd heard or seen anything strange lately."

Richards scratched his chin. "Can't say I have. Not directly. I don't go out much these days. Not since Dora took the turn. Got a nurse that comes a few times a week, food delivery every third day. I fetch the mail. That's about it."

Beretti nodded. "How long have you lived here?"

He chuckled. "Whole life. Born just down the ridge. This house belonged to my grandfather. He passed it to my folks, and then to me. Same soil. Same walls."

Beretti leaned back a little. "Ever seen anything… unusual? In the woods? Creatures that aren't exactly normal?"

Richards arched a brow. "Well now. That depends on what your version of 'unusual' is."

Beretti gave a small chuckle. "Let's say larger than a bear. Smarter than a cat."

The old man tilted his head, eyes narrowing. "You talkin' about the Hairy Man?"

Jacobi raised his eyebrows slightly. Beretti didn't move.

"Yes," she said.

Richards nodded once, like he'd expected it. "They've been here longer than we have."

"You've seen them?" Beretti asked.

He shifted in his chair and looked between them. "You

want the long or the short of it?"

Beretti didn't hesitate. "The long, please."

"Alright then. Get comfortable." He leaned back slightly, hand resting on the arm of the chair. "First time I was 'bout sixteen. Me and a buddy were huntin' out back. That'd be the south stretch, forty acres or so. Still dark when we went out. Had our gear. Walked the edge of the creek line. Something started movin' with us. Not on four legs. On two. Kept pace, just out of sight."

Jacobi sat forward, listening.

Richards continued, voice low and calm. "We made it to the tree stands. Sat up there for hours. No deer. No squirrels. Even the bugs shut up. But we kept hearin' owl calls. Same pattern. Too perfect."

He scratched his knee absently. "By midday we gave up. Climbed down, started back. Soon as we hit the trail, it followed us again. My buddy Joe spun around and caught a glimpse of it. Said he saw its head peek from the brush. Big, dark face. Tall. Eyes like coals."

"What did you do?" Jacobi asked.

"Ran. Like we'd lit a fire under our boots. Heard it

followin' us. Big steps. Too darn big."

He pointed to the floor. "Burst through that door like the devil was chasin' us. My mother was in the kitchen. She just nodded and said, 'Told you not to mess with the Hairy Man.' Never doubted her again."

Beretti tilted her head. "You've seen more since?"

"A few. Mostly glimpses at the tree line. Heard them plenty though. They knock on trees, holler like someone dyin'. But they never hurt us. Not once. Not even when they came close to the house. Used to leave apples on the edge of the yard sometimes. They'd take them. Never left a mess. Always careful."

He paused.

"But then Red Eyes showed up."

Beretti didn't hide the shift in her tone. "Who was Red Eyes?"

Richards's face darkened. The light from the window caught the lines on his jaw, deep and worn.

"Ugliest and meanest creature I ever laid eyes on," he said. "Saw it twice. Never want to again."

Jacobi leaned forward. "Can you describe it?"

Richards hesitated. "Alright."

"Chestnut hair. Not like the others. Long and thick. Two streaks of silver down the back of its head like someone painted it. Bigger than the rest. At least nine feet tall, maybe ten. Arms like tree trunks. Built like *William 'The Refrigerator' Perry* was glued together three times."

He glanced between them, then sat back a little, like the memory had crept up from somewhere he'd tried to bury.

"First time was back in... oh-two, I think. I was drivin' home from town with Dora. Took the scenic route because she always loved that stretch. We were headin' down that gravel road west of the creek, just as the light was startin' to fade. I saw movement out in the field and figured it was just a deer."

He swallowed, the memory close enough to shadow his features.

"But then the darn thing stood up."

"It moved as if it had no bones, rising up from the earth in one smooth motion. I slowed the truck. Looked right at it. Thing turned its head and just stared. And its face... Lord. It looked unnatural. As if it was made by someone who had only heard a description of a face but never seen one."

He shivered and rubbed his arm. "Then it did something I'll never forget. It smiled, or maybe snarled. I couldn't tell. But its face contorted, twisted into somethin' so ugly I had nightmares for months. My Dora screamed, and I hit the gas."

He fell quiet.

Jacobi and Beretti didn't speak. The air in the room felt denser somehow.

Finally, Richards looked at them again. His voice had gone softer as he shot a quick look over at Dora.

"That was the first time. The second…"

He let out a long sigh and rubbed his face with one hand.

"That was about twenty years ago when Red Eyes killed the couple up the road. They had the same last name as the sheriff…" He paused, thinking. "Beretti."

CHAPTER 1

Beretti flinched, a quiet gasp escaping before she could stop it.

Jacobi turned to her, then back at Richards. He understood instantly. This wasn't just any story. Richards was talking about her parents.

Beretti didn't say a word.

The old man kept going, unaware.

"They lived about a half mile up that way," he said, nodding toward the east-facing window. "Had a lovely little place. Nice folks. And a daughter, light hair, just like yours, dear."

He pointed at Beretti with a faint, crooked smile.

"Geez, that kid was a bit of a wild one. Always runnin'

around barefoot, chasing something or other. Smiled like the world couldn't touch her."

He frowned slightly and looked down. "For some reason, I could never remember her name. Always just called her Peanut. She'd always giggle every time I'd call her that."

He shook his head, then continued. "They had their share of trouble though, the Beretti's. The father, Daniel, I think… he was gone a lot. Military man. So it was mostly just Diana and the girl around. Sheriff used to stop by now and then. I think he and Daniel were brothers or cousins, something like that. Of course he wasn't the sheriff then, though."

Richards scratched the side of his nose. "I get to ramblin'. Memories are like stubborn goats. Gotta wrangle 'em before they disappear again."

He gave a dry chuckle, then shifted in his seat.

"You can stop me anytime. I know I ramble, but I don't get much opportunity to talk to folks these days."

He pulled at a loose thread on the knee of his pants, eyes down, voice quieter for a beat.

"As I was saying, they'd had run-ins with the Hairy Men. And not just the males. I think there were some females too. I warned Diana once. Told her I saw one of them creatures just standin' still beside the shed. Watching Peanut on the porch like it had all the time in the world. Gave me the damn chills, it did."

Beretti didn't move. Her hands stayed folded in her lap, one finger tapping lightly against the back of the other.

"I slowed down when I saw it. Thought maybe I was seein' things. But no. It was there. Big. Still as a statue. The girl, she never saw it. Just kept playin' with her dolls."

He inhaled deeply and leaned back. "I had a talk with Daniel after that. He said he'd seen them plenty of times. Claimed they had a particular interest in the girl. He kept a shotgun by the front door and said his wife was a good shot too. He told me they'd been harassed worse than most folks around here."

Jacobi watched as Richards's tone shifted.

"Said they'd go quiet for a while, then come back hard. Bangin' on the walls, runnin' across the roof at night. Found handprints on the windows. The truck doors would be left open come morning. Just harrasin' them ya know?"

He rubbed his hands together slowly. "Hell, the man tried everything he could think of. Put up more lights around the house, cleared away the shrubs so they couldn't hide close. Said it helped for a little while, but not enough."

Jacobi shot a glance at Beretti. Her face had gone still, her eyes glassy and locked on Richards. She wasn't blinking much.

"I think Daniel shot at them a few times," the old man went on. "Didn't kill any, but maybe it kept them at bay for a spell. But they'd always return. He said it got worse as the girl grew up. Like they were waiting for something."

Richards's expression changed again. The muscles in his jaw shifted under his weathered skin.

"Diana caught Red Eyes peering through her daughter's window one night. Said it just stood there, staring while the girl slept. The damn thing had to hunch to even fit its face in the frame. She nearly fainted right there. After that, she wouldn't step outside after dark unless Daniel was right beside her with the twelve-gauge."

He paused again, mouth pressed into a thin line.

Jacobi stayed silent, looking over at her every now and then.

Beretti's focus was locked on the old man, like she was

tracking every word, every breath.

He could sense the emotions shifting beneath her calm. Grief, suspicion, maybe even anger. But she held herself together. He felt for her, but he knew she wanted the truth. Needed it.

Richards looked between them and blinked, oblivious. "Bless her heart. She was a good mom, Diana. Real protective. She tried to shield that girl from it all, but I think it wore her down. I could see it in her face that last year."

And still, Richards didn't see it. Didn't know that the woman sitting across from him was the child from his memory. The one he'd seen dancing barefoot on that porch. The one whose life had twisted in the shadows of something monstrous.

He looked between them, eyes damp and flickering, unsure if he should go on.

"Not a nice story. You want me to stop?"

Beretti didn't blink. "Please continue." Her voice was flat, almost quiet.

Richards gave a small nod, then went on.

"Alright then. It happened just before dusk, if I remember correctly," he said. "Diana had made a pie for Dora and me. Said she was going to drop it by after supper, but I told her not to fuss. Figured I'd walk up and get it myself. Good air, stretch the legs. Dora was napping, and it was too nice of an evening to waste. Thank God she stayed home."

He shifted in his seat, eyes narrowing slightly.

"Daniel and Diana were out near the cars when I got there. He was fixin' something on his truck. Diana had the pie in a little basket. I remember she had flour still on her hands. Funny what your mind keeps hold of."

"Diana mentioned their little girl... damn, what was her name? It's right there on the tip of my tongue. Anyway, she said they'd sent Peanut off for a few days while they figured out what to do about Red Eyes. Smart move. Probably saved her life."

He exhaled, slow and uneven. "I can see it like it was yesterday. We were just standing there talking when I felt it. You know that feeling, like someone just dropped ice down your back? That kind of cold. Then Daniel **turned his head**, and I saw his whole body lock up."

Richards looked past them then, as if seeing it unfold

again through a window only he could look through.

"It was standing in the treeline. Red Eyes. Still as a stone, just... staring. The look on its face... it was like pure hatred. You could feel it coming off him, thick as smoke. Why, I don't know, but I think we all knew, deep down, it wasn't just watching this time. It had a plan. It came with something in its mind, and it was gonna see it through."

Richards's voice lowered, the edge of it trembling.

"Then it moved. Like a blur at first, but in slow motion. It dropped to all fours and came charging toward us. On all fours, can you believe it? Mouth open, snarling like a rabid beast."

His voice faltered. "Daniel fired. Full blast. I heard the shot, saw the muzzle flash, but it didn't even flinch. Just kept coming like it didn't feel a thing. Like it was too far gone to care."

"We were closer to the cars than the house, so Daniel shouted for us to get in. We ran. Diana and I got into her car. Daniel slid behind the wheel. He floored it down the drive."

He went quiet for a moment, throat working around something too old and heavy to spit out easily. His hands were trembling. He noticed, frowned, and took each one in turn, gripping them to still the shake.

"We were just about to hit the main road when it caught up. Slammed into the back of the car like a battering ram. The whole thing pitched sideways. We went into the ditch, hard. I hit my head against the door. Lights went out."

He rubbed his temple, the skin under his eyes darker now.

"When I came to, it was chaos. Screaming. Metal twisting. I couldn't move. My ribs were broken. Felt like I was breathing through a straw."

He looked down at his hands.

"Daniel was already gone. Red Eyes had pulled him through the windshield, I think. I don't know what it did to him. Diana was screaming, trying to get out. Then it got her too. Tore through the windshield too, I guess."

His voice cracked. "It tried to reach me. But the roof... the impact must've crushed it just enough. It couldn't get to me. Just kept trying, pawing at the metal, snarling."

Jacobi sat frozen, gaze darting toward Beretti. She hadn't moved. Her expression was unreadable, like she'd placed herself on a shelf far away from the moment.

Richards cleared his throat, quieter now.

"I don't remember anything else until I woke up in the hospital. They told me someone found the wreck, called it in. I never saw her again. Peanut. But I do think of her every now and then."

"Geez, I got carried away, didn't I? The only person I ever told that story to was Dora. Well, not all of it. She didn't want to hear the ugly parts."

He glanced over at her then, softened for a second, and took a breath.

"I tried telling the sheriff it was Red Eyes, but he shut me down quick. Told me to keep my mouth shut. Dora was running a little clothing shop in town back then, and he said if word got out, he'd see to it she lost it."

"A few years later, Dora let something slip to a friend and it started to spread. Sheriff tore strips off me for that. Warned me again, loud and clear. He was a real piece of work. Retired to Florida, thank God. They can have him."

Beretti stood suddenly. Her voice was tight, held together by force, with something raw just under the surface. "Thank you for telling the truth."

She didn't wait for a reply. She turned and crossed the room in quick strides, like she was trying to outrun the story itself. The door creaked open, then closed shut behind her.

Jacobi stood, slower, watching her go. He turned to Richards.

"Thank you for your time, sir." His voice was calm, respectful. "Ma'am," he added with a gentle smile toward Dora, who sat unmoving in her recliner, her eyes still fixed on the faded screen.

Richards looked at him, puzzled. His brow pinched. Something stirred behind his eyes, like a thought almost caught but slipping through the cracks.

"I... I hope I didn't upset the lady," he said, voice faltering. "Didn't mean nothin' by it. I just... sometimes I talk too much."

Jacobi gave a small, understanding nod. "You told the truth. That matters more than you realize."

"You take care now," Richards mumbled.

"You too," Jacobi said, then turned and stepped out into the brightening morning.

CHAPTER 2

The door of the SUV slammed shut behind Jacobi as he climbed into the passenger seat. The engine rumbled steadily, the cabin already warm from the heater running. Beretti didn't look at him.

Before he could even reach for his seatbelt, she threw the vehicle into reverse and backed hard out of the narrow driveway. The tires squealed against the old concrete as she whipped them around toward the main road.

Jacobi braced a hand lightly against the door. His eyes flicked over to her, but she didn't meet his gaze. Her shoulders were rigid, her hands gripping the wheel in a hold so stiff it looked painful. The set of her mouth was grim, a stubborn line carved deep.

He watched the landscape whip by, trees blurring at the edges of his vision. The ride was fast, jerky. Like she wanted to be anywhere but here or crawl out of her own skin.

He opened his mouth once. Shut it again.

What could you even say after something like that?

"I…" He tried again, his voice low. "Are you alright?"

No answer.

"Beretti." He kept it gentle. "You don't have to talk about it. But if you want to…"

Still nothing.

"I get it was a lot. Anyone would be rattled. But this was about your…"

"No," she snapped.

He blinked. "I just think…"

"I said no."

Her voice cracked through the cabin, raw and final. It was a warning, one he recognized but disliked obeying.

They rounded a bend fast. Jacobi caught the brief flicker of houses passing by, then the turn onto Ben's street. Leoni's car was parked in the driveway. One of the dogs barked once from somewhere inside.

Beretti pulled into the driveway but left the engine running.

Jacobi turned toward her, uncertain. "Maybe you should…"

"Get out."

He stared at her. "What?"

"Out. Now."

He frowned. "Come on, Nicole. Talk to me. I can help you."

She turned sharply toward him then, her face pale but fierce. "Get the fuck out, Jacobi."

The SUV seemed to pulse with her anger.

He hesitated for a heartbeat, reading the storm behind her expression. Then he nodded once, quietly. Without another word, he popped the door open and stepped out onto the cracked driveway.

The second he cleared the door, she slammed it into reverse and peeled down the street, the SUV vanishing into the gray morning haze.

Jacobi stood there a moment, his chest heavy. He hated feeling powerless. Hated seeing her hurting and not being able to fix it.

He walked up to the house and knocked twice.

Leoni opened the door almost immediately, Whiskey wagging her tail at her side.

Leoni's eyes narrowed slightly in concern. "Hey... where's Nicole?"

Jacobi stepped inside, running a hand down his face. "She took off."

Leoni frowned. "Why?"

He exhaled. "She's upset."

They moved into the kitchen. Leoni set down the dish towel she had been folding. Wink circled Jacobi once, sensing the tension, before hopping onto his favorite chair.

"What happened?" Leoni asked, voice low.

Jacobi leaned against the counter, feeling the weight of the morning settle between his shoulders. "We spoke to a man who knew her parents. He told us the real story about what happened that night."

Leoni's brow creased. "Real story? I thought they were in a car accident."

Jacobi shook his head once. "Ben told you that. Because that's what everyone was told. But there's more."

Leoni stayed quiet, waiting.

He explained it simply, without embellishment. About Red Eyes. About the years of harassment. About the final night. How her parents had fought so hard to protect her. How they had sent her away for a few days, a move that probably saved her life.

By the end, Leoni's hand was pressed lightly over her mouth and tears flowed down her cheek.

"She heard all of that?" she whispered.

Jacobi nodded.

"She just sat there," he said quietly. "Didn't blink. Didn't speak. Just took it all in."

Leoni sank into a kitchen chair. "She was already carrying a lot. But this..."

Jacobi signed. "Yeah."

Leoni studied him for a long moment. "And you?"

He shrugged. "Tried to get her to talk. She wasn't ready."

"She told you to get out?"

"Yeah."

Leoni smiled sadly. "But you're still here."

Jacobi looked toward the door like he could still catch sight of the SUV somewhere down the road.

"I'm not going anywhere."

Outside, the cold morning light edged into the yard, washing the street in pale silver. No cars moved. No sound cut the stillness beyond a distant crow cawing once from the trees.

The world felt muted.

Inside the kitchen, Jacobi settled onto the chair opposite Leoni, waiting for Beretti.

Nicole would come back.

When she was ready.

CHAPTER 3

The black SUV sped along the empty road, passing a flock of birds that scattered from a stretch of roadkill up ahead.

Beretti didn't remember pulling out of Blackridge. One minute she was tearing down Ben's street, the next she was halfway through town, the buildings blurring past her windows in a colorless smear. The SUV thrummed beneath her, every mile pulling her farther from what she'd just heard and deeper into what came next.

She hit the call button on the dash.

Ben's name lit up.

The line picked up after two rings.

"Hey, Kiddo," he said.

Beretti didn't waste time. "Did you know?"

A pause.

Ben's tone changed. "Nicole... know what?"

"That my parents were killed by a Sasquatch."

The silence stretched. Not hesitation. Not disbelief. Just heaviness.

Her voice was low, controlled. She didn't wait any longer for an answer. "Thought so."

She ended the call before he could speak again.

Her reflection in the driver's side window looked ghostlike, skin pale, lips pressed flat, eyes glossy. She hated that she could feel the sting of tears. They hadn't fallen yet, but they waited.

She pulled off the road and parked, letting the engine idle. Leaned forward, elbows resting against the wheel. Her shoulders dropped slightly. Her head bowed.

Killed.

Not in an accident.

Not a freak event.

Hunted. Taken. Gone.

By the kind of thing she'd dedicated her life to tracking down.

She tried to remember the days before it happened. Her mother, Diana. Always strong, firm in her tone but gentle with her eyes. Had there been a clue? A look of fear? A warning she'd missed?

Beretti thought back. There had been something. That trip. The one to the coast with Ben. She hadn't questioned it at the time. She was a kid. Just excited to leave town. Diana had packed her things, told her to have fun with her uncle, and kissed her on the head. There'd been something in her mother's expression, restrained, sad. Had she known?

They must have.

They'd sent her away to protect her.

The thought twisted in her stomach.

She bit the inside of her cheek, hard. Tried to block it out. She wasn't going to fall apart. Not here. Not now.

She sat up and put the SUV back in drive. The tires spat

grit as she rejoined the road. Ahead, a T-section approached, and she slowed.

Left led deeper into nowhere.

Right would take her to the coast.

She turned the wheel abruptly, made a clean U-turn, and pointed the SUV back toward town.

A short while later, she pulled in at a small storefront. She stepped inside without looking at anyone. Just got what she came for and left.

Less than two minutes. A brown paper bag tucked under her arm.

She climbed back in, shut the door, reversed, and pulled onto the road again.

The SUV gained speed, the trees slipping past. The bag sat untouched beside her on the seat. The windows were down just enough for the cold to keep her alert.

CHAPTER 4

1 88 Blackcrow Lane hadn't been touched in two decades. The overgrown drive swallowed the SUV as Beretti eased it forward, tires rolling over fallen branches and the brittle remnants of leaves long dead. The structure ahead was cloaked in shadow, tall grass bending around it like fingers trying to reclaim what had once been part of a family.

As she pulled to a stop, two deer bolted from the edge of the trees, startled by the noise. They vanished into the brush with a crash of hooves and snapping undergrowth, and the clearing stilled again.

Beretti shut off the engine and sat for a moment. The stillness pressed in, dense and unmoving. It felt like the past had crept in through the seams, waiting for her to step outside.

She grabbed the brown bag from the passenger seat,

reached inside, and pulled out the bottle of vodka. She twisted the cap and took a long swig, letting the burn settle in her throat before opening the door and stepping out.

The breeze bit at her skin, but she barely noticed.

The yard was frozen in time, with untamed grass, rusted garden tools leaning against a shed, and a swing hanging crooked from the back porch beam. Her father's old Bronco still sat in the drive, tires soft and body streaked with grime, as if it had been waiting all this time.

The house was a single-story shell, its paint faded to a dull off-white and windows clouded by age and weather. Some shutters hung askew. One was missing entirely.

She took another drink and started walking.

The earth felt soft under her boots. Not muddy. Just tired. She passed by the old oak tree at the edge of the field, the one she used to climb. The tire swing her father hung from one of its branches still dangled there, limp and gray. She touched it with one hand and let it sway.

The field behind the house opened wide. Weeds tangled themselves high, some chest-level, some broken and browned. She made her way into the middle of it, ignoring the brush scratching her jeans, and lowered herself into the grass.

She lay back slowly, her head against the cool earth, the sky stretching above her. Gray clouds floated low and distant. For a long time, she didn't move. Just let herself be still.

Wind moved through the weeds, whispering secrets she wasn't ready to hear.

She remembered the last time she saw the house. The memory had lived in a locked room inside her for twenty years. But now, the door had been blown open, and everything inside came crawling out.

Her mother's laughter in the kitchen. The hum of the old fridge that kicked on and off like a heartbeat. Her father's boots in the hallway, heavy and familiar. Her own voice echoing down the hallways as she chased after their shepherd mix, Blue. That dog never stayed still, always knew when her mood shifted. He'd curl up at her feet when she was quiet, nudge her arm when she tried not to cry.

She wiped at her face with the sleeve of her jacket. It came away damp.

Beretti sat up slowly and stood. Her legs were stiff, her back sore from the cold ground. She took another swig from the bottle and headed toward the porch.

The wooden steps groaned beneath her weight. The paint

had long since flaked away, leaving only gray wood and rusted nails. Cobwebs laced the corners of the overhang. She reached for the doorknob and tried it.

Locked.

Of course it was.

Beretti stepped back, braced herself, and kicked.

The door cracked inward with a sharp splinter of sound. One more kick sent it flying open, slamming into the wall behind it.

Silence returned.

She stepped inside.

The air was thick with dust and something stale. The smell of time. Cobwebs shimmered in the dim light, stretched from corners like gauze. Dust floated in the air, disturbed by her arrival.

She didn't rush.

Her boots tapped across the scuffed hardwood as she moved from room to room. The blue couch still sat in the living room, cushions faded, a coat of dust blanketing every surface. She reached out and ran her fingers along the edge of the armrest. Her old spot. The end seat. She used to curl there with a blanket wrapped around her knees, her mother beside her with a book.

Her fingers trembled slightly.

The television was still there, an old box model that had once been the center of their evenings. The remote sat on the armrest, as if waiting for someone to pick it up again.

She walked slowly into the hallway. The walls lined with pictures now dulled with grime. Her hand brushed one, a photo of her, around eight, missing a front tooth and holding a fishing rod too big for her.

She stopped outside her old bedroom. The door stood half-open. She pushed it gently.

Inside, the bed was still made. A faded quilt stretched over it. She stepped in, ran her hand over the dresser where she used to keep her treasures, magazines, rocks, drawings, a broken locket with her parents' photo tucked inside.

But she couldn't stay in that room. Not yet.

She backed out and turned toward the kitchen.

That was the room that hurt the most.

The light from the small window fell across the counter, highlighting a baking pan still sitting out, its surface dust-covered, but unmistakably one of her mother's. The faint scent of flour and time lingered faintly beneath the age.

The fridge stood against the wall, its surface covered in magnets and faded school papers. Beretti pulled it open. Empty. Someone had cleaned it out long ago, removing what would spoil, but left everything else untouched.

She let it fall shut and leaned against it, sliding down until she was seated on the cold floor. The bottle sat between her knees. She reached for it, lifted it, and drank deeply.

Tears came before she could stop them.

Soundless at first. Then harder. She buried her face in her arm and let it happen.

Twenty years of pain cracked open in the quiet of that kitchen. Her shoulders shook. She didn't try to stop it. She didn't hold herself together this time.

She sank to the floor, arms wrapped tight around herself, and began to rock, the sobs tearing through her in waves.

They stole her breath. Made her gasp like she was drowning.

The memories didn't stop. Her mother's voice calling her in for dinner. Her dad teaching her how to clean a fish. A night she'd been scared of a noise outside and he sat up with her until morning.

All of it. Every thread of joy tangled with the horror of how it ended.

And still she cried, not caring who might hear, not caring that for once she wasn't in control.

Beretti pressed the bottle to her forehead, the glass cool against her burning skin. Her breath came in broken pieces.

She didn't want to forgive anyone. Not Ben. Not the universe. Not the thing that had taken them. Not herself.

Not yet.

Eventually, the sobs faded.

But she didn't move.

She just sat there. On the floor. In the house that had raised her. In the last place her family had been whole.

And for the first time in a long time, she let herself grieve.

CHAPTER 5

Jacobi paced the living room, his steps soft against the hardwood floor. Outside, the midday light spilled in through the windows, stretching hazy and gold across the furniture.

Wink lay on his back near the couch, one paw twitching now and then. He cracked a lazy eye open to watch Jacobi pass again before rolling over and letting out a long, dog-sized sigh.

The front door clicked open. Leoni stepped back inside, brushing a bit of windblown hair from her face. Whiskey trotted in beside her, tail wagging slow and steady.

"We just did a slow lap around the block," Leoni said, her voice quiet but steady. "She mostly sniffed and strutted like she's still got speed."

Jacobi managed a weak smile but didn't stop pacing. His

eyes flicked toward the window.

Leoni crossed the room and hung up her coat. She turned and leaned on the kitchen counter, watching him for a moment.

"You want a coffee?" she asked.

He nodded. "Yeah. Strong one, please."

She set to it. The machine gurgled and hissed, and the familiar scent of brewing coffee filled the space. She didn't speak until she slid the mug across the counter.

"She'll be okay."

Jacobi took the mug and nodded, though he wasn't sure he believed it.

"I know.," he said. "I am just worried about her."

"It is clear you care for her."

"I do."

Leoni folded her arms, watching him. "She has let you in as much as she feels is safe. That means something."

Jacobi stared into his coffee for a beat before answering.

"Usually we're part of a team, right? Apex rotates people in and out depending on the job. But these past few months it's just been us. We've had to lean on each other. We've built something out of that."

"Not many people can say they've earned her trust," Leoni said softly.

"She carries too much," Jacobi said. "I don't think I realized just how much until today."

Whiskey let out a sharp bark, jolting Wink into a confused roll. A moment later, Ben came in through the front door. His face was shadowed, his steps heavy. He looked like a man worn thin by more than just the morning behind him.

Leoni turned toward him. "Did you find her?"

Ben shook his head and pulled off his coat. "No. After she called me, I drove around looking for her."

He draped the coat over a chair and walked toward them, stopping just short of the couch. Wink circled Ben's feet before settling again.

"She called you? What did she say?" Jacobi asked.

"She wanted to know if I knew."

"And?"

Ben sank into the armchair. "I didn't... not right away. Back when it happened, the story was just the car crash. That was enough to get people to stop asking questions. I took it at face value too. For a while."

Jacobi leaned forward. "But something didn't feel right."

"No. Some things didn't add up. So I started looking where most folks didn't bother to look. And eventually I found the truth."

Leoni sat down beside him but didn't speak.

"Why didn't you tell her?" Jacobi asked.

Ben shook his head. "She was already grieving. Lost everything. Then she started drifting, getting into fights, hanging with the wrong people. I didn't think she could handle the truth back then. And when she joined the military, I figured... let her move on. Let her build something new. Why pull her back into the dark?"

Jacobi's voice was even. "Makes sense, I guess."

Ben nodded. "Yeah. But I don't blame her for how she took it."

"She dropped me off here and peeled out like she was escaping the truth." Jacobi said, running a hand through his hair.

Ben exhaled slowly. "She probably was."

The room went still for a few beats. Whiskey hopped up onto the recliner and curled up, her ears twitching as she settled.

Leoni glanced at Jacobi. "Do you have any idea where she went?"

"No," he said. "She didn't say."

"She'll come back when she's ready," Leoni said gently. "She's always found her way back before."

Ben nodded. "That is true."

Jacobi looked toward the window. "Any reports come in today? Anyone see anything?"

Ben shook his head. "Not a thing. Quiet. Too quiet maybe."

Jacobi sipped his coffee, set the mug down. "Tonight might be different."

"Could be," Ben said.

"Guess we just play the waiting game then." Jacobi said, finally sitting down on the couch.

CHAPTER 6

Ben sat at the kitchen table, finishing off the last bite of a sandwich when his phone buzzed. He wiped his fingers on a napkin, glanced at the screen, and answered.

"Sheriff Beretti."

He listened for a moment, frowning. "Alright, Clay. Just stay inside and keep an ear on it. We'll head your way."

He ended the call and pushed back from the table, heading into the living room where Jacobi sat on the couch, thumbing through emails on his phone.

"That was Clay Darrow," Ben said. "Says something's tearing through the back of his property. Screams, howls, trees snapping."

Jacobi grabbed his jacket. "You want backup?"

Ben's mouth tugged into a dry half-smile. "Thought you'd never ask."

Jacobi stood, grabbing his gear bag from where it sat by the door. "Hell yeah. Let's go see what kind of mess we've got this time."

They moved into the kitchen where Leoni was setting down two mugs. She looked up, reading Ben's expression instantly.

"Be careful out there," she said, stepping forward.

Ben leaned down and pressed a kiss to her forehead. "Always."

Jacobi gave her a small grin. "We'll be back soon. Hopefully in one piece."

Leoni waved them off, but her eyes followed them to the door.

Outside, the midday sun was weak behind a thick overcast sky. The wind carried a chill, and the sheriff's cruiser waited at the curb. They climbed in and pulled away without another word, tires whispering over the asphalt.

The drive to Clay's place was quiet. Both men were too

keyed up for casual talk.

When they pulled up the long dirt driveway, Clay met them at the door but refused to come out onto the porch.

"I ain't goin' out there," he said, voice trembling. "It sounds like a war back in them trees."

Jacobi narrowed his eyes. "I thought you and Jolene were heading out of town for a few days."

Clay glanced back into the house and gave a quick shake of his head. "We were supposed to go yesterday. Had to push it back as Jolene's niece had emergency surgery. She didn't want to leave town until we knew her niece was okay. We'll be going this afternoon now. Ain't no way we are staying any longer."

Ben nodded. "Stay inside. Keep your doors locked. We'll check back in with you."

Jacobi turned, listening.

From somewhere deep behind the property, the sounds drifted in.

A heavy crash. A scream tore through the air, raw and primal, something that didn't belong in the natural world.

The sound of wood splintering followed, sharp as a crack of lightning.

Jacobi flinched, the sound crawling under his skin.

Ben popped open the back of the cruiser and pulled out the drone case. He started to open it, but Jacobi gestured.

"I've got it," Jacobi said. "You keep eyes on the feed. I'll get it in the air."

They moved quickly to the open field just past the house, the wind tugging at their jackets. Jacobi crouched and unpacked the drone efficiently, launching it in a steady hum of rotors.

He handed Ben the second iPad and tapped the screen. "Here. You're on the live feed. Tap here to switch views, and here if you need to zoom. Just keep an eye on it and call out anything that stands out."

"Okay," Ben replied, eyes already locked on the display.

Jacobi controlled the drone, angling it north. On the screen, the thermal feed bloomed to life in vivid, pulsing outlines against a sea of cold.

"Here we go..." Jacobi mumbled. "Got movement. Five

heat signatures. They're just now coming through the trees. That must've been the commotion Clay heard."

Ben leaned in.

On the screen, three lean shapes darted through the forest's edge, hunched and fast. They twisted between trees with unnatural speed, arms sweeping wide as they ran. Tall and rangy, with long snouts and angular shoulders, the Dogmen reached a rocky outcropping that jutted above a clearing and came to a halt, panting, eyes scanning the woods behind them.

Seconds later, two towering figures surged from the brush. Thicker, broader. The Sasquatch. Their strides were longer, more grounded, but every step pushed them forward with undeniable force. Their hair bristled, one of them streaked with something darker near the shoulder, possibly already wounded.

The Dogmen turned, teeth bared. There was no escape.

Both sides stared across the rocks and grass, chests heaving. A charge built in the air. One of the Dogmen barked and dropped to all fours, claws digging into the dirt. Then, silence. Every creature crouched. Muscles coiled.

The smallest Dogman sprang first, claws out, jaws

snapping. It leapt at the larger Sasquatch, but the big one met it midair, catching it around the ribs and twisting. The two slammed into the earth, rolling through broken brush. The Dogman clawed at the Sasquatch's neck, raking its shoulder with deep, bloodied swipes. The Sasquatch grunted, shifted its grip, and pinned the creature with one knee, then drove its thick hand into the Dogman's chest, again and again, each strike reverberating with impact.

The Dogman tore in half.

Its spine gave first, snapping with a sickening crunch. The torso peeled apart, sinew and organs stretching before they ripped free. Blood sprayed across the clearing in heavy arcs. The upper half dropped with a wet slap, entrails spilling onto the leaves. Its lower half hit the ground a beat later, twitching once before going still.

The remaining two Dogmen bolted.

They sprinted for the trees and leapt into the lower branches of a pine, climbing fast, claws raking deep into the bark. They settled high in the canopy, snarling, crouched and ready to strike again.

The larger Sasquatch barreled forward and slammed its fists into the trunk. Bark exploded outward. The whole tree shuddered. The smaller Sasquatch picked up a large rock and hurled it upward. It crashed through a cluster of branches. Another followed, smashing into the forked base of the limbs above.

A third rock struck one of the Dogmen in the shoulder. It yelped and dropped several feet, scrambling to regain its hold. It failed.

The creature fell, twisting midair. It landed hard. The impact knocked the wind out of it.

The larger Sasquatch pounced, driving the creature into the ground. It tried to bite, but the Sasquatch shifted and smashed its face sideways with a forearm. Then it lifted the Dogman and slammed it down again, cracking the earth with the blow.

The smaller Sasquatch threw another rock, this one striking the remaining Dogman in the thigh. It fell next, trying to land in a crouch, but the moment it did, the larger Sasquatch turned and grabbed it by the back of the head, dragging it backwards.

The Dogman lashed out, scoring the Sasquatch's thigh with its claws, but the hit was shallow. The Sasquatch roared and flung the Dogman into a nearby tree. The creature bounced off, dazed.

The smaller Sasquatch moved in. Together, they grabbed its arms and yanked it upright. Then the larger one delivered a blow directly to its chest that echoed like a battering ram. The Dogman collapsed to its knees.

The second Sasquatch grabbed the Dogman's head and slammed it to the ground. The skull cracked. A final stomp crushed it fully.

Blood leaked into the dirt, pooling beneath the twisted limbs.

Both Sasquatch were breathing heavily, wounded but standing. Blood soaked their arms, stained their fur. One had a deep gash across its ribs. The other limped slightly but kept its posture straight.

Jacobi stared at the screen. "They're hurt."

Ben nodded. "But they made damn sure none of them got away."

The Sasquatch dragged the remains of the Dogmen across the clearing. They returned for the one torn apart, carried both halves, and piled the three bodies near the edge of the road.

Then, in silence, they urinated on the corpses.

Marking them.

Without a glance back, they turned and walked into the trees.

Ben and Jacobi exchanged a look.

"Well," Ben said, "that was entertaining."

"It was something, alright," Jacobi replied.

They walked back through the field toward Clay Darrow's house. The porch light flicked on as they approached.

Clay opened the door a few inches, eyes wary.

Ben stepped forward. "We checked the area. It's handled. But you'd do well to finish packing and get out by dusk."

Clay nodded, rubbing the back of his neck. "Yeah. I got the message loud and clear."

"Good," Ben said. "Don't wait around for it to change."

They returned to the cruiser. The engine rumbled to life, and they drove the short distance to the spot where the bodies lay.

Jacobi stepped out and pulled out his phone. He moved a few paces away and made the call.

What was left of the bodies was barely recognizable.

"At least that's three down," Ben said quietly.

Jacobi returned to his side. "By my count, there's only one left."

Ben stared out into the forest. "I hope that's true."

CHAPTER 7

Ben was driving back home, relaying some half-finished story about getting his boot stuck in a cattle grate during a high school dare. Jacobi laughed, quietly shaking his head at the image, when the radio buzzed.

He picked up the call and responded, "Sheriff Beretti."

The voice on the other end was shaky, strained with panic. "Sheriff, we've got a situation. Little boy gone missing off Pelham Road. Backyard runs right into the woods. He's autistic and non-speaking. Mom says she dozed off for twenty minutes. Woke up, and he was gone."

Ben was already up from the table. "How long's he been gone?"

"She noticed twenty minutes ago. Could've been earlier."

"Call everyone in. Tell the deputies to bring their rifles. I want everyone armed before we step into those woods."

He hung up and turned. Jacobi sat in the passenger seat, rifle pack already in the footwell at his feet. "What's going on?"

"Kid's missing near the woods. Autistic. Non-speaking. The house backs right onto the tree line."

Jacobi responded. "When it rains, it pours."

It was around 3 p.m. when they arrived. Several vehicles were already parked along the gravel shoulder outside a small, worn house. A woman stood wrapped in a blanket near the porch, her face pale and drawn. Ben approached her first, speaking low. "I'm Sheriff Beretti. We're here to help find your son." "Ma'am, can you tell me exactly what he was wearing when you last saw him, and give me a physical description?"

She swallowed hard and wiped at her cheek. "Red long-sleeved shirt, gray pants. No shoes. Brown hair, brown eyes. Last time I measured him, he was about four foot one."

"No jacket?"

She shook her head. "He doesn't like to wear heavy things. Gets annoyed if I try to make him wear them."

"Does he wander off often?"

"No. Never. Not like this."

Ben placed a hand gently on her shoulder. "We're going to find him."

A woman stepped forward from the group of neighbors and wrapped her arms around the mother, whispering something quietly as the mother began to cry. Ben gave them a moment before turning and walking to the gathered group.

A few neighbors were gathered along the edge of the property, quiet, and tense. Deputies moved in tight circles, some checking maps, others gathering equipment.

Ben stepped into the center of the group and raised his voice just enough to carry. "We've got a seven-year-old boy with autism. Mason Petrovic. Last seen wearing a red long-sleeved shirt, gray pants, no shoes. Brown hair, brown eyes, about four foot one."

He pointed toward the treeline. "The forest behind the house slopes into ravines and runs dense for at least two miles. There's a creek about three-quarters of a mile down the main gully. We're setting up a grid. Everyone goes in pairs, no exceptions. We've had more predator sightings than usual this past week, so stay alert and report anything unusual right away. Each team takes a radio, check in every fifteen. We've only got a few hours of daylight left, so move with purpose."

He passed out radios from a case in the back of his truck, then pointed to two deputies. "You two sweep the western trail. Samuels and Carter, take the old firebreak. Watch for tracks. He may be moving or he may be still. He may not respond to his name."

Jacobi stood slightly apart from the group, eyes already on the treeline. He adjusted the strap on his rifle, his posture alert but loose.

Ben approached and lowered his voice. "We'll take the ravine trail."

Jacobi nodded and turned toward the woods without hesitation. "We should split off once we get past the ridge. If he's moving, we cover more ground that way."

Ben hesitated a beat before nodding. "Alright. Just keep your radio on."

Jacobi looked at him. "Trust me."

The woods closed around them. The cold clung to the earth, seeping into their boots. Each step forward felt absorbed by the undergrowth. Jacobi moved with unwavering attention, rifle in hand, eyes constantly shifting from the trail ahead to the scattered signs left behind. The forest was still, but not in a restful way. It was a quiet waiting. Listening. Like it knew something they didn't.

"Mason!" Ben called, low and firm.

No answer.

Jacobi crouched beside a patch of disturbed earth. "Hold up," he said.

A small footprint, bare. The toes curled slightly at the edge. A smear of something red nearby.

"Jam," Jacobi murmured. He touched it, felt the faint stickiness still clinging to the leaves.

Ben stepped beside him. "He came this way."

Jacobi nodded. "Yeah. But he wasn't alone."

He gestured toward a much larger print a few feet away, half-sunken into the pine needles. Wider than a man's, flat with five distinct splayed toes.

"Not Dogman," he said. "Too flat. No claw marks. But big."

Ben didn't speak. He didn't need to.

Jacobi rose. "I'll follow this line. You swing north. Something about this feels off."

"You sure you want to split?"

Jacobi was already moving. "I've got it."

Ben watched him disappear into the underbrush.

Jacobi moved deeper into the forest, following a faint path broken by low branches and pressed-down ferns. The light had shifted overhead. Duller. More silver than gold. The farther he went, the more the trees seemed to lean in. Sounds were swallowed up. Even his own breath seemed quieter here.

He followed the trail until it broke over a narrow ridge and dipped into a shallow gully, damp and strewn with slick roots. A dragging mark cut through the mud. Just beyond it, a small handprint, smeared at the edge. Then, a second one. Larger. Heavy. Pressed into the slope as if someone had crouched there, watching.

Jacobi crouched and studied the prints, trying to gauge the size, the pressure. There were scuffs on nearby bark. Fresh breaks on thin saplings. He shifted his rifle to one hand and continued down.

Ten more minutes passed. Nothing. No sound, no sign. Then, he heard something faint. Not words. Not footsteps. A repetitive, soft noise. Jacobi followed it.

Just beyond a twist of dense shrubs, in a hollow surrounded by stones and old roots, he found him.

Mason.

The boy was kneeling in a patch of moss, his head rocking slightly from side to side. His fingers tapped his thighs in a rapid, repeating rhythm. A low hum buzzed in his throat. He didn't seem afraid. Detached maybe. Focused inward.

Jacobi didn't move. He scanned the area around the boy first. A thick print dented the soft earth behind him. Wide. Deep. No shoe tread. No claws. He followed the impressions with his eyes, noting the direction. Whoever had made them was gone. But not long ago.

The air was thick with the overwhelming stench of old garbage and wet dog.

He could feel it. That sense of being watched. It settled at the base of his neck and stayed there.

Jacobi stepped forward slowly, lowering himself so he wouldn't tower. "Hey there, Mason."

The boy didn't respond. Just kept humming, rocking slightly.

Jacobi slung the rifle and inched forward. When he reached out and gently touched the boy's shoulder, Mason tensed but didn't pull away. His voice hitched but didn't rise.

Jacobi lifted him carefully. Mason clung tighter than expected, his face pressed against Jacobi's chest, fingers fisting into the fabric of his jacket. The boy was humming again, a soft, shaky pattern that buzzed against his ribs.

Then a sharp cackle rang out from the ridge to their right.

Jacobi froze for a beat, head snapping toward the ridge. It was a high-pitched cackle, too loud for a coyote. The Dogman.

He shifted the boy higher against his chest and took off at a quick pace, boots slipping on the moss-slicked ground. The slope fought him. Roots snagged at his steps. His breath turned rough.

Behind him, something crashed through the trees.

Another cackle.

Then came the unmistakable pounding of something else, heavier, faster. Trees groaned. Limbs snapped. Something massive was moving through the undergrowth, not toward him, but toward the Dogman's path.

Jacobi didn't look back.

He assumed the second set of footsteps belonged to the Sasquatch. Hopefully it would deal with the Dogman before he had to.

He pushed on, branches lashing at his arms as he barreled through the forest.

The boy began humming louder, his body rocking. Jacobi said a quiet reassurance, eyes scanning for the break in the trees that marked the edge of the gully.

He angled left, avoiding a downed trunk, and saw a patch of light through the canopy ahead.

Jacobi pushed through a wall of brush, lungs burning.

Voices shouted in the distance.

"Jacobi!"

Ben.

"I've got him!" Jacobi called.

The trees thinned. Ben and two deputies met him at the edge.

Ben took the boy. Mason didn't let go easily. His fingers held Jacobi's coat a second too long before releasing.

Jacobi staggered back, rifle in one hand, chest heaving.

CHAPTER 8

The sun had dipped lower by the time they climbed into the sheriff's cruiser. Ben was driving, the inside of the vehicle quiet aside from the soft crackle of static from the radio.

After a minute, Ben glanced over. "You did good out there."

Jacobi leaned back in the seat, watching the trees blur past the window. "Just did what needed doing."

"No, I mean it," Ben said. "You've got good instincts. Not many would've pushed that far in alone. And you didn't panic."

Jacobi exhaled slowly. "It wasn't just me. The Sasquatch saved our asses."

Ben blinked. "You sure?"

"Positive," Jacobi said. "It took off after the Dogman. Gave us the opening we needed."

Ben shook his head slowly, keeping his eyes on the road. "I've been around a long time. Never thought I'd be grateful to one of those things."

Jacobi gave a faint, tired chuckle. "Neither did I."

They were nearly back when Ben's phone buzzed. He tapped the accept button on the dash and said, "Beretti."

"Hey, it's me," Leoni said. "I heard something happened out by Pelham Road. Everything okay?"

"Yes, it is," Ben said. "Jacobi found the boy. Safe."

There was a pause, followed by a soft exhale. "Thank God. I was hoping that's what I'd hear."

Ben let the quiet settle a moment, then she added, "I already ordered dinner, by the way. Thai, could you please pick it up on your way home? You know the place I like."

Ben gave a small, tired smile. "Of course. See you soon."

Ben ended the call and rested his hand briefly on the console, headlights cutting through the early evening haze.

He glanced over at Jacobi. "Hope you like Thai."

Jacobi gave a tired shrug. "I like everything."

CHAPTER 9

The truck's headlights cut a narrow path along the cracked service road, their beams dull against the creeping dusk. Crickets buzzed over the low hum of tension lines overhead, and the sky had shifted to a bruised purple. A breeze moved through the trees with just enough force to rustle the higher branches. Somewhere down the ridge, a single coyote called, its cry lost quickly in the stillness of the forest.

"Every damn time," Ray mumbled, finishing off the last of his gas station coffee. "Friday night, I'm halfway through a ribeye, and they call us out. Clockwork."

"Probably didn't want to pay the overnight crew double," Marcus said as he stepped onto the lift and tightened his harness. He was taller than Ray, thinner too, with a quiet voice that often made people lean in to hear him. "And you're always halfway through a ribeye."

Ray climbed on after him, mumbling under his breath. "You know what I mean. Some of us got lives, man."

"Mmhmm. Lives that involve meat and the same bar stool at Duffy's."

The lift creaked upward, the platform rising beside the cracked pine pole. It was an old install, gray with weather, splintered in places. The streetlight farther down the road was dead, like the rest of the line.

"You got the voltage probe?" Ray asked, squinting up at the insulator.

"Should be in the red bag," Marcus said, leaning over the transformer casing. "Looks like a junction crack. Nothing major. Just enough to arc when the temperature shifts."

"Wouldn't crack at all if they'd replaced this junk when we told them to," Ray mumbled.

Marcus reached into the bag, rifled through it, then stopped. "You didn't grab the probe, did you?"

Ray gave him a look. "I thought you packed the tools."

"You were in the truck last."

Ray sighed like it was the greatest burden in the world.

"Fine. I'll go get it. Don't go falling off the pole or nothing."

He lowered the lift and stepped off once it hit the gravel, still mumbling as he made his way to the rear of the truck. The utility door swung open with a dull clunk, and he leaned inside, moving aside coils of wire and old fuse boxes.

"Genius forgets the damn probe," he said to himself. "Bet Marcus planned this, just so he could stand up there and do nothing."

A rustle came from across the narrow road. Not leaves shifting. Something else. Heavier. Slower.

Ray stopped. He straightened, listening. Nothing. No footsteps, no wind.

He leaned partway out, scanning the trees. The darkness had thickened, shadows deepening beneath the branches. Everything stood still.

He called out, "You see anything up there? Hear that?"

Marcus turned and looked down. "See what? No. Just you mumbling. What'd you hear?"

Ray glanced at the trees again. "Thought it was something in the woods. Probably a deer."

"You want me to come down and hold your hand?"

"Bite me," Ray said, turning back into the truck.

He grabbed the red tool bag and dug around until he found the voltage probe wedged beneath a vest.

"Of course," he said. "Right where I left it."

He stood up, half-closed the compartment, and turned toward the lift.

Then he stopped.

Something was moving at the edge of the light, just beyond the reach of the beams. It crept along the gravel, low and slow.

For a second, he thought it was a trick of the shadows. But it kept moving.

Ray stepped out from the truck and squinted. Whatever it was, it moved with a smoothness that didn't sit right.

"Marcus," he called. "Get down. Now."

Marcus moved fast. He unclipped from the cross-arm, then began climbing down, his gaffs digging into the pole, one boot below the other.

"What's going on?" he called.

"Just get in the truck. Might be a bear."

That got him moving quicker. Ray didn't take his eyes off the shape.

It wasn't walking like a bear. Too lean. Too calculated.

Marcus jogged over. "Where?"

Ray pointed. The thing had stopped.

In the hazy yellow light, its outline became clearer. It was big. Too big. Shoulders broad, waist narrow, arms too long for the body, limbs angled wrong. It crouched just inside the shadow.

"That's not a bear," Marcus said quietly.

Then it stood.

Straightened slowly. No rush.

As it rose, something in its joints gave a deep, brittle pop, like bones cracking back into place after being bent too long.

It shifted its balance like it had done it a hundred times before.

Man-shaped, almost. But something wasn't right. The legs bent the wrong way. The arms hung too low. The head was narrow, and the ears pricked forward.

Ray backed into the truck, almost stumbling.

Marcus didn't move, eyes wide. "What the hell is that?"

The creature tilted its head and stared. Its eyes gave off a faint amber glow, not reflection, something internal.

It sniffed the air, slowly.

Ray grabbed Marcus by the jacket and yanked. "Get in. Now."

They dove into the cab and slammed the doors shut.

The creature didn't run. It didn't flinch. It just stood there and watched.

Ray's hand fumbled for the key.

"Start it," Marcus said, voice tight. "Start the damn truck."

The engine caught, rumbling to life.

Outside, the creature lowered itself to all fours and slipped back into the woods without a sound.

Ray stared after it, his hands still on the wheel.

"We're not reporting this," he said.

"Hell no."

CHAPTER 10

The cab was quiet, every tick of the engine loud in the silence. Outside, a breeze stirred the leaves. Ray sat with both hands on the wheel, staring hard into the treeline like he was daring it to move. Marcus leaned back in the passenger seat, arms folded tight, jaw clenched.

"So... we leaving or what?" Marcus asked.

Ray didn't answer right away. His eyes stayed locked on the darkness beyond the headlights.

"If we don't finish, we'll get flagged," Marcus added. "You know how it goes. Miss a line check, they dock half a shift."

Ray's fingers tapped the steering wheel once. "You saw that freak show too. Thing stood up. On two goddamn legs."

"I know what I saw," Marcus snapped. "But it's gone. Probably ran off the second it heard the truck start."

Ray turned toward him. "And you're just fine going back up there? With your back turned, like none of that just happened?"

Marcus threw up a hand. "What do you want me to say, man? We either finish the job or we spend the weekend filling out reports and losing pay."

Ray stared at him, jaw tight. "This is beyond reports. That thing wasn't right."

"No kidding. But it's not here now. We go up, fix it, and get out. Quick. Simple."

Ray still didn't move.

Marcus sighed hard and yanked the door handle. "Screw it. I'm not getting chewed out because you're suddenly superstitious."

Ray snorted and reached for his own door. "Fine. Let's just get this shit over with."

They stepped out and headed toward the lift. The woods felt off. The crickets had gone dead silent. The lift groaned as Marcus tapped the controls, the platform rising with slow, uneven effort.

Ray climbed on first, mumbling under his breath. Marcus joined him, hitting the panel again to bring them level with the crossbeam.

"In and out," Marcus said. "Ten minutes."

At the top, Marcus opened the junction cover while Ray held the tool bag steady between them.

"You sure you grabbed the right tool this time?" Marcus asked.

"Yeah," Ray mumbled. "Triple-checked the damn thing."

A few minutes passed. Wires snapped into place. The wind moved in short, cold bursts above them.

But Ray kept looking over his shoulder.

Marcus noticed. "You gotta quit that."

"Can't. Feels like it's still out there, watchin'."

"You're gonna freak me out, man. Just focus."

Ray bent to adjust the probe, jaw locked tight.

"You think it was a werewolf?" he asked.

Marcus didn't respond.

Ray kept going. "Mutant, rabid, I don't know. It moved like a mix between a lizard and a spider. Gave me the fuckin' creeps. And that sound it made."

"Ray, shut up."

Ray turned toward him. "I'm tellin' you, man. We saw something we weren't supposed to."

He stopped.

Went still.

"Marcus."

Marcus turned. "What?"

Ray didn't speak. He reached out, grabbed Marcus by the shoulder, and pointed down.

Marcus followed his hand.

There, in the road, directly beneath them, it stood.

The creature.

Still as stone. Upright. Those amber eyes catching the light like hot coals.

Marcus stiffened. "Oh shit."

"It's just standin' there," Ray mumbled. "Starin' us down."

"You think it's gonna jump?"

"I don't know. Maybe not. We're up high enough."

Marcus leaned over. The creature didn't move. Just watched, relishing their fear.

Ray's voice dropped. "Call someone. Now."

Marcus patted his pockets. "Shit. My phone's in the truck."

Ray cursed. "Of course it is. Mine too. Goddamn it."

They both looked back down.

The creature moved.

It stepped around the base of the pole. No sound. Just slow, steady pacing. It circled once and stopped again, eyes still locked on them.

Ray whispered, "Why the hell is it just standin' there like that?"

Marcus shook his head. "I don't know. Maybe it's sizing us up."

The thing looked up.

Then at the pole.

Marcus saw it coming. "No. No way. It's not going to…"

It jumped.

Its claws hit the pole halfway up with a heavy thump.

Ray and Marcus both screamed.

Marcus grabbed the control. Ray clutched the railing.

"Get the bucket away from the pole!"

The motor kicked in, grinding as it pulled them back.

Below, claws ripped into wood.

It was climbing.

And it was fast.

CHAPTER 11

The bucket swayed. Ray stood frozen beside Marcus, both of them gripping the railing as the machine groaned and shifted slightly. The motors were strained, whining louder than usual, as if the pressure in the air had seeped into the mechanics.

Below them, the Dogman clawed at the pole, rising foot by foot, its long arms swinging with terrifying speed and grace. Wood splintered as its claws dug in. Bits of bark rained down.

"It's climbing too fast," Marcus whispered. His voice was thin, nearly childlike.

Ray's knuckles went white. "This thing's not stopping."

"Get us away from the pole!"

"I'm trying!"

Ray slammed the side controls again. The bucket groaned and inched sideways, away from the pole, metal straining as it extended them further over the road.

For a moment, the movement seemed to help. The creature dropped down a few feet, losing grip, then disappeared into the shadows beneath.

Ray panted, wiping sweat from his forehead with the back of his wrist. "It's gone. It's gone."

"I don't see it," Marcus mumbled. He looked straight down, scanning the base of the pole. "Where the hell did it go?"

Ray turned his head, and in that instant, something slammed into the bucket.

The whole structure rocked violently. A clawed hand gripped the edge, then the other. The Dogman hauled itself over the side with inhuman strength, its muzzle twisted into a snarl, teeth gleaming with saliva.

Marcus screamed. Ray barely managed to reach for the wrench at his side before the creature lunged.

It went for Marcus first.

Its jaws closed over his shoulder, ripping deep into muscle and bone. Marcus's scream cut through the air like a siren, high-pitched and raw. Ray grabbed for him, tried to haul him back, but it was no use.

The Dogman yanked him out of the bucket with ease, like pulling a doll from a toy box.

His body sailed downward, slamming onto the gravel below with a sickening thud.

Ray backed against the control panel, eyes wide, breath ragged.

The Dogman turned to him.

Its eyes were the color of firelight, fixed on him with cold intelligence. Blood dripped from its maw, dripping onto the metal floor of the bucket.

Ray raised the wrench, hands trembling. "Stay back. You bastard, stay the hell back."

The creature tilted its head.

Then, as quickly as it had attacked, it dropped out of sight.

Ray collapsed against the side of the bucket, chest

heaving. He dared a look over the edge.

The Dogman was at Marcus's body, crouched low. It gripped him by the legs and dragged him across the gravel toward the ditch. The sounds that followed were wet and awful, each tear and crunch sharper than the last.

Ray shut his eyes. "Jesus Christ..."

He felt his stomach twist, bile rising into his throat.

From the bucket, he could see everything. The creature tore into Marcus like a wolf into a deer. There was no mercy in it, no pause, no hesitation. Only hunger. It was feeding.

Ray pressed his back to the railing, the wrench still clutched in one hand. He could hear bones breaking. He could hear the creature chewing.

He began to whisper under his breath.

"Our Father who art in heaven, hallowed be thy name..."

His voice cracked halfway through the first line.

He tried again, barely able to push the words past his lips. "Thy kingdom come, thy will be done..."

The lift creaked beneath him.

The blood on the metal floor was warm against his boots.

He couldn't stop shaking.

He stared out across the treetops, refusing to look down again. He kept whispering prayers, though the words stopped making sense. A muddled litany of pleas and fear.

Every noise below sent new panic coursing through him. Twigs snapping. Flesh tearing. Breathing.

Ray didn't know how long he sat there.

The night felt vast and close all at once, the darkness wrapping around him with no edges. In the distance, a single call echoed and faded, and for the first time, Ray felt truly alone.

The feeding stopped.

The silence that followed was worse.

Ray's mouth went dry. He didn't dare move.

Then he heard it again.

Claws scraping the pole.

It was coming back.

Ray gripped the wrench tighter, his hands slick with sweat.

"Please," he whispered. "Please, no."

The claws got louder.

The wood creaked.

He braced himself.

And then… nothing.

The sound stopped halfway up.

Ray waited. Ten seconds. Twenty.

No more scraping. No heavy breathing. No footsteps.

He leaned slowly over the side, inch by inch.

The road was empty.

Marcus's body was gone.

Only a pool of blood remained, dragged into the brush.

Ray sat down hard, pulling his knees to his chest, rocking slightly.

He didn't know if the creature had left or if it was waiting for him to climb down.

He stayed there, whispering prayers into the night, while the sky went darker and the woods waited.

CHAPTER 12

Deputy Ellis adjusted the volume on the cruiser's radio as he pulled out of the gas station, the familiar crackle giving way to soft country music. A fresh cup of black coffee sat in the holder between him and Deputy Colenar, who was already halfway through his.

"That girl of mine's on a roll this week," Colenar said, sipping. "Spelling test yesterday, got 'em all right. Then today, she tells her teacher she wants to be a veterinarian."

Ellis gave a small smile, eyes scanning the quiet street as they turned onto the main road. "Better than saying she wants to be a deputy."

Colenar chuckled. "Ain't that the truth. You?"

"Jenny's birthday's coming up. Trying to decide if I should go with the dog she's been begging for or play it safe with a trampoline."

Colenar raised his cup. "Go with the dog."

They drove in silence for a few blocks, the town still and quiet around them. A pair of kids biked past a laundromat. A neon sign buzzed outside a pizza place, its letters half-burned out.

"Alright," Ellis said, sitting straighter. "Let's make the outer pass."

Colenar nodded, setting his cup down. "Back road or the logging route?"

"Start with the old county line. Then swing through by the quarry."

The cruiser rolled over the asphalt as they left the center of town behind. The streetlamps gave way to long stretches of blacktop bordered by forest and open fields. The occasional glint of animal eyes caught in the headlights reminded them they weren't alone.

Colenar rubbed his arms. "Temperature dropped quick."

"Frost warning came in an hour ago."

They rounded a bend, trees thick to their left and a slope dropping off to the right. Up ahead, red and orange hazard lights pulsed through the trees.

Ellis slowed the cruiser.

"What the hell is that?" Colenar asked, leaning forward.

A power company truck sat parked on the shoulder, boom extended high above a cracked old pole. The bucket was occupied.

A man was up there.

He was waving, shouting something they couldn't hear yet.

Ellis brought the cruiser to a stop thirty feet back. The headlights washed over the truck and the edge of the road.

"That's one of the linemen," Colenar said. "Think he's stuck?"

Ellis didn't answer.

Colenar opened his door.

"Hold up," Ellis said sharply. His eyes moved over the treeline and back across the ditch. Nothing stirred, but every instinct in him started going off.

Colenar stepped out, foot hitting the gravel.

"Get back in the car."

Colenar turned, frowning. "Why? He's waving for help."

"Get back in the car. Now."

There was no hesitation in Ellis's voice. Colenar paused, then stepped back in and shut the door.

Ellis eased the cruiser forward. As they neared the power truck, the man in the bucket became clearer. His uniform was soaked in sweat and something darker. His face was pale. He was shouting down at them, desperate.

"Help! You gotta help me! Please!"

Colenar lowered his window just enough.

"What happened?" he called.

"Something killed Marcus! Tore him apart! It was like a fucking werewolf!"

Ellis stared. "Goddamn it."

Ray pointed toward the gravel. A pool of blood glistened where the headlights hit it. A long streak led off toward the ditch.

"I don't know where it went!" Ray yelled. "It was down there, feeding on him, then it just stopped. I don't know if it's hiding, waiting for me to come down!"

Ellis leaned out the window. "Stay where you are. Don't move. We're calling it in right now."

"Don't leave me!" Ray screamed. "Please, don't leave me up here!"

"We're not leaving," Colenar said quickly. "We're staying right here. We're just going to call for backup."

Ellis picked up the radio and keyed in. "Dispatch, this is Unit Twelve. We've got a power truck on County Line Road with one male up in a lift bucket. He says his coworker was killed by some kind of animal. Notify the sheriff and EMS, but keep EMS on hold for now. We need backup."

"Copy that, Unit Twelve," came the dispatcher's reply. "Backup en route. Standing by on EMS."

Ellis set the mic down.

Colenar glanced over. "Jesus. You think he's in shock?"

Ellis kept scanning the woods. "He saw something. And

I've got a bad feeling I know what."

Colenar turned. "Wait. You think it's the Dogman?"

Ellis gave a slow nod. "Could be."

Colenar's voice dipped. "You saw it?"

Ellis shook his head. "No. But I saw the footprints. I was with the sheriff and the FBI agents when we tracked it. That was enough."

Colenar looked back toward the woods. "You serious?"

"Dead serious."

Ray's voice cracked again from above. "It's out there. I swear it's still out there."

The bucket shifted slightly in the wind. Ray crouched down, then popped back up to check around him.

Ellis's hand hovered near his sidearm. His eyes never stopped moving.

Every bush, every branch, every shadow seemed too quiet.

And the man in the bucket kept shaking.

CHAPTER 13

The sheriff's cruiser rolled up just past the parked utility truck, headlights sweeping across the roadside ditch before cutting into the tree line. The vehicle eased to a stop, its engine ticking softly as the two front doors opened.

Ben stepped out first, shotgun held low but ready. He scanned the roadside and treeline. Jacobi climbed out a moment later, rifle at the ready.

They walked toward the other cruiser. Inside, Ellis sat with his window half-open. Jacobi gave him a nod.

"Ellis," he said. "Good to see you."

Ellis returned it. "Thanks for coming."

Jacobi's eyes shifted to the other deputy still inside. "Who's your partner?"

"Deputy Colenar," Ellis replied.

Jacobi nodded once, eyes already moving to the bucket above. Ray was crouched inside, gripping the railing, voice raised in panic.

"Get me down! Please! It's gonna come back!"

Jacobi stepped forward and called up, firm but even. "Quiet. We've got you."

Ray stopped yelling, but his breathing was ragged and loud in the stillness.

Ben looked at Ellis. "What do we have?"

"Guy up there says his coworker was ripped apart by something. Says it looked like a werewolf. He's been stuck up there since. I believe him. There's blood over there on the shoulder."

Jacobi followed Ellis' gaze to the pool of blood. "Let's get him down. Colenar, Ellis, both of you out. We'll cover the area together."

Ellis stepped out immediately. Colenar hesitated, then climbed out on the passenger side, hand resting on the grip of his sidearm.

Jacobi moved beneath the bucket and looked up again. "Ray. You're coming down now. It's clear for the moment. Hit the controls and lower slowly."

Ray fumbled at the lift panel. The machine groaned and began descending, juddering a little on the way down. He flinched with every sound, constantly looking out into the woods.

Ben circled the truck slowly, shotgun raised and ready. The road was too quiet. The breeze barely stirred the tops of the trees.

The bucket was almost down when Ellis spoke up, voice sharp.

"Oh shit. There. Over there."

Everyone turned.

Ellis pointed toward a break in the brush on the far side of the ditch. "It moved. Left to right. Just there."

Jacobi shouldered his rifle, aiming into the trees. "Anyone got eyes on it?"

Everyone said no.

Ben moved to the passenger side of the cruiser, angling

toward where Ellis had indicated. "Ray, out of the bucket. Now."

"I can't," Ray stammered. "I can't move."

Jacobi kept his rifle ready as he stepped toward the lift. "Get out, now."

Ray's legs buckled. He froze halfway over the edge of the bucket.

Jacobi swore under his breath, slung his rifle, and walked over to the bucket, reached over and grabbed Ray by the collar.

"Let go. I've got you."

Ray didn't move.

Jacobi yanked him over the side. Ray collapsed on the pavement, shaking, lips moving but not forming anything coherent.

Ben was already backing toward the cruiser. "Ellis, Colenar, get in your vehicle."

They did.

Jacobi pulled Ray to his feet and opened the back door of

the sheriff's cruiser. He pushed him inside and slammed it shut.

Something cracked in the trees.

Jacobi jumped into the passenger side and said. "Go, go, go."

Ben was already behind the wheel. He didn't wait. The cruiser lunged forward, tires gripping hard as they sped down the road.

Ray huddled in the backseat, mumbling and rocking slightly, arms wrapped tight around his chest. The light from the dashboard stuttered across his blood-spattered face.

Jacobi stared out the window, rifle resting across his lap.

"I'll return with some deputies tomorrow morning to search for your colleague, Ray. Safer that way," Ben said while looking in the rear mirror.

Ray didn't reply. Just kept rocking back and forth mumbling to himself.

CHAPTER 14

Jacobi sat hunched on the couch, elbows resting on his knees, staring at the dark TV screen. It was just past 5 a.m. The only light came from the kitchen, where one small lamp cast a low amber glow across the hardwood floor. Whiskey, the little Jack Russell cross, lay curled near his feet, snoring softly.

He hadn't really slept. Maybe drifted a little here and there, but mostly he sat up listening to every tick of the old clock on the wall, every creak of the house settling into itself.

The sound of footsteps drew his gaze to the hallway.

Ben emerged, shuffling into the room wearing flannel pajama pants, an old T-shirt, and battered slippers. His dark hair was flattened on one side like he'd wrestled with the pillow most of the night.

He stopped when he saw Jacobi.

Ben scratched his jaw and gave a low grunt. "You're up early kid, or couldn't you sleep?"

Jacobi gave a faint smile. "Couldn't sleep, I guess."

Ben sighed and dropped into the armchair across from him. His slippers tapped a slow rhythm against the floor as he sat there, a restless tension riding his frame.

"Couldn't sleep either," Ben said finally. "Too much on my mind. Nicole especially."

Jacobi nodded, pushing his palms against his knees. "Yeah. Same here."

For a few long moments, they sat there in the quiet, the house breathing around them.

Jacobi cleared his throat. "I was thinking…" He hesitated, then went on, "Would it be alright if I borrowed Leoni's Jeep for a bit?"

Ben leaned back slightly, studying him. Not judging, just taking the measure of the ask.

Without a word, he stood up and walked to the small bowl on the sideboard. He plucked out a set of keys and tossed them lightly toward Jacobi.

Jacobi caught them in one hand.

Ben pointed at him, voice dry. "Don't scratch it. That thing's her favorite toy."

Jacobi grinned, the first real one in days. "No promises, but I'll do my best."

Ben gave a grunt that might've been a laugh and rubbed his face with both hands, the weight of worry clinging to him like a second skin.

Jacobi rose, slipping the keys into his jacket pocket.

"Thanks, Ben. You heading out to look for Ray's coworker soon?"

Ben acknowledged him, the lines around his eyes deepening. "Yeah. We will be ok. I have two deputies coming with me."

Jacobi ran a hand through his hair and headed for the door. "Okay. Give me a call if you need help."

Whiskey perked up, then settled back down when she realized he wasn't going anywhere fun.

"Go find our girl," Ben said quietly.

"I'll try," Jacobi replied, before stepping out into the cool morning air. He had no plan, but he was finally doing something.

CHAPTER 15

The town was still asleep, its homes tucked behind trees and frost-dusted yards. Only the birds had started their day, calling softly from the pines as Jacobi slowed at a faded intersection. A soft band of light stretched across the treetops, thin and cold through the haze.

He tapped the brakes, glancing left and right. Nothing but endless trees and empty fields.

He drummed his fingers on the steering wheel, thinking.

Where would she go?

If he were Nicole Beretti, furious, hurting, needing space but too stubborn to say so, where would he hide?

The answer came quick, solid and certain.

He shifted into drive and made a right.

A few miles up, just as he started to settle into the drive, two deer burst from the tree line and bolted across the road. Jacobi cursed and slammed the brakes, the Jeep jolting hard enough to throw him against the seatbelt.

Before he could breathe, the whole herd followed.

Hooves flashed. Fur blurred. One of the deer hit the hood with a heavy thud, scrambled clumsily, and vaulted off into the trees.

Jacobi stared at the fresh dents now carved into the Jeep's front end.

"You gotta be fucking kidding me," he mumbled, throwing his hands up.

He could already picture Leoni's face when he would have to tell her.

Well. Technically, *he* hadn't scratched it.

He sighed and pressed on, rolling slower now.

He passed Ole Man Richards property, its roof sagging in the morning light.

A little farther up, maybe half a mile, he spotted it: a nearly invisible driveway, half-eaten by undergrowth and trees leaning in tight from both sides.

Jacobi turned in.

The Jeep crunched carefully over old gravel and moss. The farmhouse emerged gradually from the trees, hunched and worn from time.

Peeling paint. Battered windows. A place forgotten by the living.

But nestled awkwardly near the porch was a familiar black SUV.

A knot formed in his stomach.

He parked behind her vehicle and shut off the engine.

For a moment he sat still, hands resting on the wheel. He wasn't sure what he would find inside, or what he was even supposed to say when he did. Every part of him felt out of his depth. But he wasn't going to sit there and wait for clarity.

He pushed the door open and stepped into the cold. The air smelled of damp wood, rusted metal, and the faint musk of hay left too long in the rain.

He scanned the yard first. The field beyond the tree line was still and empty, dotted with tufts of frost and brittle grass. Nothing moved. No sign of anyone.

Then he saw the door.

It hung crooked on its frame, the wood around the lock splintered and pushed inward.

Jacobi's hand moved instinctively to his sidearm.

He stepped forward slowly, every movement cautious and alert.

Inside, the house was dim and frozen in time. Dust floated thick in the dim light. The furniture sat sagging under years of neglect, and the air held the quiet ache of old memories.

He cleared the front room with focus watching for any movement.

Then he stepped into the kitchen and there she was.

Beretti lay curled on the cracked linoleum, her arm bent under her head. A bottle of vodka lay loosely in one hand.

Jacobi exhaled hard and holstered his weapon.

He crossed the kitchen quickly, heart dragging low in his chest, and crouched beside her. Her breathing was steady, slow. She was out cold.

He stood again and stepped quietly into the hallway, opening a narrow linen cupboard tucked between the kitchen and bathroom. It looked untouched, its shelves still stacked with neatly folded sheets and blankets. He pulled one free, soft with age but clean enough, and returned to her side. Gently, he draped it over her.

Carefully, Jacobi lowered himself onto the floor beside her, the cold linoleum soaking into his back. He lay there, staring up at the cracked ceiling, listening to the deep silence of the house.

No words. No lectures.

Just quiet.

Just being there.

The morning light edged through the broken doorway, painting long faded streaks across the worn floorboards. Somewhere far off, a rooster called out, thin and scratchy.

Jacobi turned his head slightly toward her.

"You're allowed to fall apart sometimes, Beretti," he said, voice barely above a whisper. "You don't have to carry it all."

She didn't stir.

He lay there a little longer, watching the dust spin lazily above them.

She looked so small like this. Small and tired and human, not the unbreakable agent she usually projected to the world.

He closed his eyes for a minute and breathed in slow.

It hurt, seeing her like this. But he understood it.

She wasn't weak.

She was wounded.

And even the toughest steel bent under enough pressure.

He reached out and gently nudged the vodka bottle away from her hand, setting it a few feet farther from her. Then he folded his hands behind his head and stared at the ceiling again.

"We'll figure it out," he said softly. "You're not alone."

Not anymore.

CHAPTER 16

A nudge at his shoulder dragged Jacobi from sleep. He blinked into the muted light and found Beretti crouched beside him, her expression groggy but clear.

"Morning," she said, voice rough.

Jacobi rubbed a hand over his face, heart catching up to reality. He glanced around the kitchen, then up at her again. "How you feeling?"

She sat back on her heels, picking up the half-empty vodka bottle and grimacing. "Alright. My head's another story though."

Jacobi pushed himself up slowly. His joints cracked from sleeping on the cold floor. He watched as Beretti set the bottle on the counter, shaking her head.

"Anything happen while I was gone?" she asked.

He stood, brushing dust from his jeans.

"Uh...yeah. Quite a bit," he said. "Ben and I responded to a call at Clay Darrow's place. Heard one hell of a fight. We watched two Sasquatch take down three Dogmen."

Beretti frowned. "I thought Clay was leaving town?" Jacobi nodded. "Yeah. They got delayed. Jolene's niece ended up in the hospital. Emergency surgery."

"After that," he continued, "we searched for a missing boy who'd wandered off into the forest. I found him, and it looked like a Sasquatch had been with him."

"Really?" Beretti asked.

"Yep. Then, as we were walking out, I heard a Dogman coming down the ridge straight for us. Next thing I know, I hear what I think was the Sasquatch running after it. Gave me enough time to get the kid out."

He paused, then added, "Also, a linesman was killed the last night out by the old access road. His coworker's in the hospital. Shock so bad they still can't get a full statement out of him."

"Wow. So much happened, and I wasn't there to help you. Not that you needed it, clearly." She said looking at Jacobi with a half a smile.

"It's been a crazy forty-eight hours alright," he replied.

She looked around the room, then leaned back against the counter again, arms folded this time. Her posture was casual, but her face wasn't.

"I've been trying to remember," she said. "Anything. The days before it happened. Something that might explain why they were targeted. A sound. A face. Anything."

Jacobi didn't speak. He gave her the space.

"I knew they were around," she went on. "Sasquatch. I just never thought it was that bad. I never thought it was that dangerous. I was a kid, but not stupid."

Her voice thinned. "And yet, I can't recall a damn thing leading up to it. Just this giant hole where the worst part of my life should be."

She looked at Jacobi, but it was like she wasn't really seeing him.

"I used to think they abandoned me," she said. "For a long time, that's how it felt. I'd run through every possibility in my head. But nothing ever fit. So I settled on abandonment. It felt the easiest way to handle it. With anger."

Her hands clenched into fists against her sides.

"But all they did was try and protect me. And I was mad at them for leaving. I carried that around like a damn anchor for years."

Jacobi sat down on the edge of the couch and leaned forward, elbows on his knees.

"You think maybe this job... this life... you got into it for that reason. Even if you didn't know it at the time?"

Beretti looked at him, her expression guarded.

He held her gaze. "You spent your career chasing down things that most people don't believe exist. Things that hurt people and disappeared into the dark. Maybe some part of you always knew. Even if the details were buried."

She didn't answer right away. When she did, her voice was quieter.

"I used to have this feeling. Just this... pressure, I guess. Like the story I was told wasn't the full one."

She exhaled deeply. "But I never imagined this. I never imagined my parents being torn apart by something we barely understand."

Jacobi didn't say anything. He knew better.

Beretti looked toward the sink, unfocused. "And my mom, all those nights she asked me to sleep in her bed... I used to think she just missed my dad. But now I think she was scared. Maybe she heard things outside. Maybe she knew something was watching. And maybe she didn't want me in my own room because she wasn't sure she could get to me in time."

She rubbed her hands together slowly. "They must've been terrified. Trying to keep a roof over our heads, pretending everything was normal, while some freakin' Sasquatch stalked our house."

Her voice wavered, but she pressed through it.

"I didn't see the enormity of it. I was too wrapped up in my own little world. And I carried that anger like it made me strong. But it didn't. It just got in the way."

Jacobi leaned back a little, watching her. "You're seeing it now. You're doing something about it."

"That doesn't fix the past."

"No. But it puts something solid under your feet. And that counts for more than you think."

Beretti lowered herself onto the couch next to him. She leaned forward, elbows on her knees, mirroring his posture.

"I keep thinking about what I'd say to them," she said. "If I could. After all this. Not an apology. Just... I don't know. Something honest."

Jacobi nodded. "Maybe that's what all this is."

She didn't say anything for a while. Just sat with it.

Then she stood. "You ready to go?"

"Yeah," he said, rising to his feet.

They worked together to lift the sagging door back into its frame. It wouldn't hold, but it gave the illusion of closure.

Beretti lingered on the porch with her hands in her jacket pockets, eyes scanning the trees and sky. The house behind them sagged against the morning light.

"Doesn't feel haunted anymore," she said.

Jacobi said nothing. He understood hearing the truth had changed something in her.

She turned and walked with him to the Jeep.

Inside, she frowned, pointing at the hood. "What the hell happened there?"

Jacobi winced. "Deer."

"Deer?" she repeated.

"Whole herd. One of them used the Jeep as a trampoline."

Beretti chuckled. "Leoni's gonna kill you."

"I know," he said, starting the engine.

They rolled down the overgrown driveway in silence, the house vanishing behind them.

After a few miles, Beretti spoke again. "What did Ward say?"

"I didn't call him."

She looked over at him. "You didn't?"

"Figured you needed space. Not protocol. Not someone trying to make this clean and tidy before you even caught your breath."

Beretti reached over and squeezed his arm. "Thanks."

"You don't have to thank me."

"Yes, I do. And for coming to get me."

Jacobi smiled a little.

She looked out the window again. Her voice was soft. "My mom used to say... your blood's worth bottling."

Jacobi smirked. "That a compliment?"

"The highest one."

The Jeep rumbled on, the trees thinning, the sky lightening with the early rise of day.

For the first time in a long time, they weren't running from the truth.

CHAPTER 17

The house was quieter than usual when Beretti stepped through the door. She smelled coffee lingering faintly in the air, heard the soft snoring of the dogs.

Ben sat at the kitchen table, elbows resting on the wood, a mug cupped between his hands. He wore his usual work clothes, but his boots were off, set neatly by the door. He looked up when she entered.

"Hey, kiddo," he said, voice low.

Beretti dropped her keys on the counter, hesitated, then crossed the room and pulled out a chair across from him. She sat, keeping her hands flat against the cool surface of the table.

"You got a minute?" she asked.

"For you? Always."

Taking a deep breath, she steadied her nerves. "How did you know the truth, Ben? About what happened to them."

Slowly, he leaned back in his chair, massaging the tense muscles at the nape of his neck. His eyes, usually bright and quick, dulled with the weight of memory.

"A few years after it happened," he said, voice quiet, "I started hearin' whispers. Little things. Things that didn't add up to what the official report said."

Beretti listened.

"I knew I wasn't gonna get the truth from the sheriff back then. Man wouldn't have told me if I put a gun to his head. So I went another way."

"There was a deputy. Younger guy, green back then. He was on scene that night. I figured he might talk if the circumstances were right."

"And?" Beretti asked.

Ben continued. "We went to the bar without a name. Had a few beers. More than a few. And sure enough, once he was good and drunk, he started spillin' it."

Beretti felt her stomach do backflips but kept her face still.

"He told me what Ole Man Richards saw that night. Told me about Red Eyes. About the wreck. About what was left behind."

Her voice cracked slightly when she asked, "Why didn't you tell me?"

Ben looked at her, really looked, and Beretti saw the regret sitting heavy in his eyes.

"You were already carrying so much, kiddo," he said. "Grieving. Acting out. Hanging with kids that weren't good for you. And when you said you wanted to enlist…" He shook his head slowly. "I figured if I laid that truth on you, it might break you. Or worse, it might make you even more reckless."

She stared at him, feeling the ache claw up her throat.

"I thought I'd tell you someday," he said. "Or maybe not at all, if life turned out alright for you. When you joined the Jaegers… when you started hunting cryptids… I thought maybe it was the universe's way of making something right outta all that wrong."

Beretti sat back, feeling the chair creak under her.

She wanted to scream. She wanted to punch the table. Instead, she just closed her eyes for a second, then opened them again.

"I get it," she said finally. "I hate how I found out. But... I get it."

Ben nodded once, a sharp bob of his head like it hurt to move. His eyes were glassy, brimming but unspilled, and he blinked hard like that might keep it together.

Beretti swallowed, her voice rough when she spoke again. "Did my mom send me away because of Red Eyes?"

Ben's mouth tightened, and he looked away, out the window at the slowly brightening sky.

"Yeah," he said. "They were getting worried. She thought it was better if you weren't there. Just for a few days, until they figured out a plan. I told her I'd take you to the coast for the weekend. Give them space to sort it."

Beretti dropped her gaze to the table.

"I don't think they ever imagined it would go the way it did," Ben said. "Hell, I didn't. They were used to the Hairy Folk acting strange, harassing, but... Red Eyes was different. Meaner. Smarter. They thought maybe a few shots in the air, maybe even moving would fix it."

She pressed her fingertips to her temple, the memory pushing at the edges.

"You were the best thing that ever happened to me after they were gone," she said finally, voice low.

Ben reached across the table and squeezed her hand. His rough palm dwarfed hers, warm and steady.

"*You are* the best thing that ever happened to me too," he said.

They sat there like that for a while, the old clock ticking off seconds like heartbeats.

Finally, Beretti pulled her hand back, clearing her throat roughly.

"I guess I got some ghosts to put to rest," she said.

Ben gave her a small, sad smile. "We all do, kiddo. We all do."

Outside, the town slowly woke up around them, unaware of the war brewing in the forests at its edges.

Inside, Nicole Beretti squared her shoulders.

One ghost down.

A hell of a lot more to go.

CHAPTER 18

The house was quiet except for the low crackle of the fireplace in the living room. Dinner dishes sat stacked neatly in the kitchen sink. Ben stretched out in the recliner, one arm draped over the side as he listened to Beretti and Jacobi tossing ideas back and forth about the remaining Dogman.

Jacobi leaned forward on the couch, elbows on his knees. "If it's wounded after that fight with the Squatch, it'll either hunker down or get desperate."

"Desperate's worse," Ben said without opening his eyes.

Beretti shifted against the armrest, tapping her thumb lightly against her knee. "We need to be ready either way. No more surprises."

Leoni walked into the room, wiping her hands on a towel. She looked between them and smiled. "How about y'all take a break from plotting death and destruction? They're lighting up the big tree on Main Street tonight. Carols, cocoa, the works."

Jacobi sat back and looked at Beretti.

"Could use a break," he said.

Ben cracked one eye open. "Wouldn't kill us to be part of the living for a minute."

Beretti shrugged, standing. "Fine. But I'm still bringing my sidearm."

Ben grunted in approval. "Wouldn't expect anything less."

They all headed to their rooms to grab jackets. Beretti strapped on her Glock, slipping her jacket over it. Jacobi did the same, checking the weight at his hip. Ben tugged on his old canvas coat, adjusting it until it sat just right.

Leoni grabbed her own coat from the hook by the door. "Everyone ready?"

"Ready," Beretti said, pushing open the front door.

The cool evening air rolled in, crisp and edged with the scent of wood smoke from the neighborhood's chimneys. The last smear of twilight was fading behind the hills, and the streetlights flickered on, casting long pools of yellow across the sidewalks.

They walked slowly, the sound of their boots and shoes quiet against the pavement. The town glowed softly under strings of lights wound around lampposts and draped across storefronts. More people appeared ahead of them, bundled in scarves and heavy jackets, chatting as they headed toward the town square.

Jacobi glanced around, taking it all in. "Almost feels normal."

Beretti nodded but kept her eyes moving, ever watchful.

A large crowd was already gathered in the square by the giant Christmas tree. The tree itself towered over the square, wrapped thick with multicolored lights and shining ornaments. Children ran laughing between the adults, chasing each other with candy canes.

From a small stage to the right of the tree, the first notes of *"Silent Night"* floated out, carried by the chilly breeze. A group of townsfolk, young and old, stood holding songbooks and singing, their breath misting in the cold air.

Ben tipped his hat a little lower against the breeze. "Hell, if I didn't know better, I'd say nothing bad ever happened here."

Leoni bumped his arm gently. "That's the point. We don't let the darkness win."

Jacobi shoved his hands into his pockets, watching a little girl twirl in her puffy jacket near the tree. "Good reminder."

They drifted toward the edge of the crowd, standing close enough to take it in but far enough to keep their eyes on everything.

Beretti felt a pang somewhere deep. This was the kind of scene her parents would have brought her to once. Back before everything shattered.

Jacobi leaned toward her slightly. "You alright?"

She nodded. "Yeah. Just... thinking."

He didn't push. They just stood together, listening to the carols, the music spreading through the town.

Ben shifted beside them, scanning the crowd almost unconsciously. "A lot of folks out tonight."

"Good thing," Beretti said. "They deserve a little peace."

Leoni pulled a thermos from her purse and took a sip. "Anyone want cocoa?"

Jacobi chuckled. "Always."

She passed it around, and for a few minutes, they stood there in silence, sipping cocoa and letting themselves be part of something whole and unbroken.

A boy tripped over his own feet and landed in the grass near the sidewalk. He popped up laughing, brushing off his jacket. His friends laughed and pointed.

Ben smiled faintly. "Kids are tougher than they look."

Beretti watched, feeling the knot in her chest loosen just a little.

CHAPTER 19

The Dogman had spent most of the day circling the outskirts, sniffing for the right trail. Its brothers and sisters had fallen to the Sasquatch, torn apart or crushed into the earth. But not it. It was smarter. Faster. More cunning. Now it would answer blood with blood.

The wind brought a tangle of smells from the valley below. The shifting masses of creatures that moved in tight herds. Nothing it wanted. Nothing worth the effort.

It had waited. Patient. Still. Eyes watching from high above as the town stirred. It did not know the names for what it saw. Did not need them. It understood motion, rhythm and scent. And today, it searched for one scent alone.

The sky had dulled from gray to a bruised yellow as evening crept in. From its perch on a rocky rise, the Dogman stayed crouched and still, its nostrils twitching with every gust. The wind cut through its coat, but it remained focused. Still as stone.

The hours passed.

Twice, it moved to investigate passing trails. Once a deer. Once something smaller. It let both go. Wrong direction. Wrong scent. It curled back into the rocks, eyes narrowing.

Then, just as the light began to fade behind the trees, it found it.

That stench. Thick. Rank. Unmistakable.

A tall one.

Even from this distance, it turned the Dogman's stomach. Filthy creatures. Their scent clung to everything. Like rot. Like earth soaked through with something old and sour. It hated them. Hated the way they moved. Hated the strength in them.

But this one was young. That much was clear. The scent was raw and thin around the edges, not settled like the elders. There was no other nearby. No warning musk. No layered trails. It was alone.

It almost smiled.

The Dogman rose from the rocks and began the slow descent. It crept between stone and root, letting gravity and instinct guide its steps. It did not rush. That was not the plan. It wanted to be noticed.

Closer now, it circled downwind, letting its scent stretch out ahead of it. It flexed its claws and dragged them across its thigh, just enough to open the skin. Blood welled and ran. The strong scent would do the rest.

It began to limp. Slow. A predator pretending to be prey.

It paused often, turning its head just enough. Glancing behind.

The wind shifted.

And somewhere not far behind, the tall one caught the trail.

Good.

Let it follow.

The Dogman could already hear it. The rhythmic crunch of footsteps and branches disturbed in its wake. The tall one probably thought it was being quiet, but the Dogman's hearing betrayed every movement. It knew exactly how close it was, how fast it moved.

The younger creature's breathing was loud, uneven. Steam poured from its mouth into the cold. Its focus narrowed to the trail ahead. It didn't notice the shift in the air. The subtle change in smells. The far off sounds that did not belong to the forest. All filtered out.

The Dogman had made sure of it.

This was no chase. This was a lure.

The Dogman passed the scattered structures of the hairless ones, keeping to the gaps between them. It moved like a shadow, silent and fast, weaving through narrow spaces and ducking low when needed. Occasionally, it let the Sasquatch glimpse it. Just a flicker of dark movement through an alley, the flash of amber eyes near a doorway. Then it would vanish again, always staying just out of reach.

From behind fences and behind walls, it could hear the high-pitched barking of other canines. They had picked up its scent, but it paid them no mind. They were smaller things, loud but harmless, bound to the hairless ones by some strange loyalty. No threat. No purpose. Not part of its mission.

As it passed close to the dwellings, it slipped by strange,

unnatural shapes that carried the hairless ones. They stank of something hot and bitter, still ticking with the memory of movement. The Dogman ducked out of sight when it saw one of the hairless ones appear in a window or doorway. It had no interest in them. It had an end goal in mind, and nothing was going to keep it from reaching it.

The buildings were strange, box-like things stacked too close together, filled with noises and smells that meant nothing. But the Dogman knew how to move around them. It had done this before. It guided the young tall one deeper into the heart of the town, through the maze of stone and glass. The tall one gave chase, never realizing it was being led.

The Dogman leapt fences and scaled low rooftops, bounding from one shadow to the next. Each time it showed itself, it lingered just long enough to ensure it was seen. Then it vanished again. The young one followed, breath ragged, driven by instinct, adrenaline, and the need to prove it could drive the Dogman from its territory.

It was working.

The Dogman almost couldn't believe it. The tall one followed blindly, mindless and eager. How stupid these worthless creatures are.

As the Dogman neared the square, it could hear the hairless ones. Their noise drifted through the narrow streets ahead.

Ahead, the town square opened beneath a massive conifer. It was nearly as tall as the surrounding structures, covered in strange shapes that clung to its branches. It knew what to do.

The Dogman felt it building. The tension. The moment.

It ducked beneath it, vanishing into the deep shadow at its base.

The tall one burst from the alley seconds later, panting hard, its steps pounding the ground. It skidded to a stop in the open, turned left, then right.

Confusion rippled across its face.

Where had it gone?

Then the lights flared to life.

Every bulb blinked on at once. Reds. Greens. Golds. The star at the top beamed down like a signal flare.

For a second, the world held still.

Until the screaming began.

People scattered from the square, pulling children, knocking over cocoa stands, screaming as they sprinted for cover.

The Sasquatch froze.

Tall and massive, even for a juvenile. Exposed under the lights.

Its head turned in jerky movements, watching the panic unfold. Shouts. Footsteps. Flashing cameras. None of it made sense.

High in the tree, hidden behind thick branches, the Dogman crouched. It could feel the chaos swell. Its tongue lolled from its mouth, its eyes fixed on the shape below.

It had executed its plan well, though luck and timing had tipped things in its favor.

Across the street, an old red pickup idled at the curb.

The driver stared.

A heavyset man in a worn cap leaned out the window, breath misting in the cold.

"Well, I'll be damned," he mumbled. "I'm about to get myself a damn Bigfoot."

He reached behind the seat and pulled out a bolt-action rifle.

The click of the action startled the tall one. It turned fast, retreating a few steps. Its shoulders hunched. Its breath came faster now.

Phones were out. People were yelling. Some had already vanished into nearby shops.

The Sasquatch backed away from the lights. From the voices. From the threat it could not name.

It did not understand the weapon.

But it understood danger.

And it was too late.

CHAPTER 20

Jacobi, Beretti and Ben rounded the corner toward the town square, feet pounding against the pavement.

Beretti's head jerked up. Her gaze cut across the square.

"What the hell?" Jacobi mumbled, already moving faster.

They weaved through the chaos, pushing toward the source of the disturbance.

Near the tree, a massive figure stumbled awkwardly into view. Covered in shaggy brown hair, towering above the crowd, a young Sasquatch, its posture low, confused. Its head swiveling side to side, trying to make sense of the bright lights and screaming people.

Ben skidded to a stop beside Beretti and Jacobi. "What the hell?"

Before they could act, a loud shout rang out.

"That's a monster!"

An older man in a battered pickup threw open his door. From behind his seat, he yanked a bolt-action rifle. He leveled it clumsily toward the Sasquatch, his face wild with panic and adrenaline.

"Don't!" Beretti shouted, her voice cutting across the square.

Ben and Jacobi yelled in unison for the man to stop.

The old man squeezed the trigger.

The shot cracked like a whip. The Sasquatch jerked sideways, stumbling as the bullet tore into its upper thigh. It bellowed, a deep, pained roar that shook the air.

Another crack split the night. The second round caught it lower, a grazing shot along the backside.

People screamed even louder now.

Beretti pushed through the mass of people, heart pounding. Jacobi was right beside her. She spotted a second man, stumbling out of a hardware store nearby, a twelve-gauge shotgun gripped in his hands.

"No!" Jacobi shouted.

The man didn't hesitate. He shouldered the weapon and fired twice.

The blasts ripped through the Sasquatch's chest and neck. It sagged, knees buckling, and crumpled heavily onto the cold pavement.

For a heartbeat, the world stood still.

The square reeked of gunpowder, sweat and something worse, the bitter tang of blood.

The two men ran toward the downed creature, weapons still in hand, shouting over each other.

"I got it!" the older man screamed.

"Like hell you did," the second one barked, waving his shotgun. "You shot it in the ass. That ain't gonna kill it. I finished it!"

They stood over the fallen Sasquatch, arguing, faces flushed red with anger and adrenaline.

Ben stormed up to them, rage simmering just beneath his usually steady surface.

"Drop your weapons," he barked.

Jacobi had his sidearm drawn, held low but ready.

The two shooters froze, glancing between them.

"I said drop them!" Ben roared.

Reluctantly, the first man put his rifle down onto the pavement with a clatter. The second lowered the shotgun more slowly, glaring at Jacobi as if daring him to say something.

Jacobi stepped forward and relieved him of the weapon.

Ben pulled out two pairs of handcuffs, snapping one set onto the older man's wrists. Jacobi cuffed the second shooter without a word.

"You're both under arrest for unlawful discharge of a firearm inside town limits and reckless endangerment," Ben said grimly. "And that's just for starters."

The crowd was closing in now, some still shouting at the two men.

"You idiots!" a woman screamed. "It wasn't even hurting anyone!"

"You shot it!" a woman yelled. "It looked human, you bastard!"

"How could you shoot it?" another voice cried. "It wasn't even attacking!"

"You could've killed a kid!" someone else added.

The arrested men snarled back, protesting.

"It was a Bigfoot. It was gonna kill you all, you fools!"

"Yeah," the other man yelled at the crowd as he was led away. "What the hell were we supposed to do? Just let it walk around? Freakin' imbeciles!"

Ben and Jacobi hauled the two men to the street, trying to keep them from getting mobbed by the angry crowd.

Beretti knelt beside the fallen Sasquatch.

It was young. A little over six feet tall if it had stood upright. Barely more than a teenager in its own world. Its hair was coated with blood where the shotgun blasts had struck. Its wide dark eyes stared up at nothing.

Her hands curled into fists.

This wasn't justice. It had been fear. Stupid, blind fear.

Ben returned from securing the two men in two deputy's cruisers, his face barely restraining his fury. He looked down at the Sasquatch and shook his head slowly.

"This didn't have to happen," he said quietly.

Jacobi stood a few steps behind them, scanning the crowd, every muscle in his body coiled with tension.

Sirens wailed as Ben turned toward them, then back to Beretti and Jacobi.

"Deputies are clearing the square and surrounding area," he said.

Beretti stood slowly, her mouth set in a grim line. She wiped a hand across her face and nodded. "I will call it in and have them pick him up ASAP."

They moved quickly, efficiently, directing the crowd away from the scene as deputies walked in with flashing lights and shocked faces.

CHAPTER 21

The sheriff's office smelled like burnt coffee and old files as Beretti, Jacobi and Ben crowded around the small surveillance monitor.

Beretti leaned in, one hand steady on the desk. She clicked through the different feeds pulled from the square's cameras and nearby storefronts, her eyes sharp and focused.

"There," Jacobi said, tapping the screen.

They watched the grainy footage roll. At first, it was just the town square bathed in the faint glow of streetlights. A crowd had already gathered in front of the stage to the right of the tree, while carolers moved among them, oblivious to what was lurking nearby.

Then the figure appeared.

The Dogman sprinted across the edge of the frame,

moving low and fast, and without slowing, dove into the massive unlit Christmas tree. It disappeared among the heavy branches and decorations, vanishing into shadow.

Jacobi let out a breath. "Son of a bitch."

Seconds later, the town's Christmas lights flicked on, flooding the tree with light.

The young Sasquatch stumbled into the frame, clearly focused on something. Confused. Its head swung side to side, trying to make sense of the brightness, the noise.

People screamed. The Sasquatch froze, trapped in a sudden sea of light and sound.

The chaos spiraled.

Jacobi shifted his weight, crossing his arms over his chest. "You're telling me none of us noticed that thing slip into the damn tree?"

Ben shook his head, his face hard. "Too dark. Too much goin' on. And everyone was looking at the mayor count down, I guess."

Beretti sat up straighter, a knot pulling tight in her chest.

"That bastard planned this," she said, voice low. "It lured

the Squatch into town. It baited it."

Jacobi ran a hand through his hair. "That's what I was thinking."

Beretti nodded. "That Dogman didn't just happen to run into a Christmas tree. It drew the Sasquatch near the people and then hid. It got lucky when the lights came on and stunned it."

Ben grunted. "Used the town. Used the people. All of it."

Beretti leaned closer to the monitor, her fingers flying over the controls. She fast-forwarded the footage, flipping through different camera angles, looking for a glimpse of movement. The square started clearing. The footage showed one shooter raise his weapon and fire, followed by the second a heartbeat later. Seconds later, Jacobi and Ben appeared, moving in fast to disarm and arrest the men. Beretti watched herself kneel beside the fallen Sasquatch.

The tree stood, undisturbed.

Until just over an hour later, after the body had been taken away.

"There," Beretti said, freezing the frame.

They leaned in together.

A dark, low shape slithered out of the base of the tree. The Dogman. It paused at the edge of the square, its head swiveling left and right. Then, quick as a blink, it sprinted into the dark street and vanished into the night.

Jacobi let out a low whistle. "It was there the whole damn time."

Ben shook his head slowly, like he couldn't believe what he was seeing. "We were yards away."

Beretti mumbled, "We were standing there... and it was right under our noses."

Jacobi threw his hands up in the air. "You gotta be kidding me."

Ben shaking his head, replied. "That thing's not just smart. It's dangerous smart. Cunning."

Beretti stared at the screen, anger burning under her skin. "Unbelievable."

Jacobi leaned against the desk. "It knew exactly what it was doing. Knew the Squatch would follow. Knew the people would panic. That's next level insane."

Ben's face was grim. "Most folks ran like they should've. But those two idiots? First thing they did was reach for their guns. Just needed the right fool to fire first."

Beretti didn't move, her voice calm but iron-hard. "And the Dogman got exactly what it wanted."

Jacobi stared at the frozen image of the Dogman on the screen, the curve of its spine low and stalking.

"We've been playing checkers," he said quietly. "It's playing chess."

Beretti clicked the screen off and leaned back in her chair.

"Well," she said, her mouth twisting in a bitter half-smile. "Time to change the rules."

CHAPTER 22

They were back at Ben's house, the kitchen lit bright as they huddled around the table. Maps and reports were spread out across the surface.

Beretti pressed the cap off the marker and made another red dot.

"Alright," she said quietly. "Darrow's field. Here." She marked it with a precise dot, then drew a line down to another point.

"Then here," she mumbled. "The parking lot attack."

Ben shifted slightly, his chair creaking under his weight. "Who could forget?"

Beretti nodded grimly and added the festival grounds to the map.

"Here. Where the woman was attacked after getting off her bike."

She tapped another spot.

She moved the marker slightly west. "Barbara's house. Not far from Darrow's."

Dot.

"And here's Ted Hoover's place. Same side of town."

Another dot.

She added a new mark farther east. "This is where the young boy was found and Jacobi heard the Dogman."

Then another, farther south near the service road. "And here. This is where the linesman was killed."

Then she tapped a point near the ridge where they had seen the first real confrontation between the Sasquatch and the Dogmen.

Jacobi leaned in closer. "That a pattern?"

Beretti sat back slowly, twirling the marker between her fingers. "Looks like a triangle," she said. "Not random at all."

Ben rubbed his forehead and looked closer. "Son of a bitch. It's deliberate."

Jacobi frowned. "Territory?"

Beretti's voice stayed low, almost distracted. "More than that. This wasn't random movement. It looks like it was the Dogmen's original plan. Pressure points. Herding tactics. Keeping the Sasquatch reactive, off balance."

Ben's eyes narrowed. "And now that most of the Dogmen are gone?"

Beretti sighed. "We're assuming there's only one left. And he's likely to stick to what's already been set up. Same triangle. Same pattern. Patrolling it. Defending it."

Jacobi rested his knuckles lightly against the table. "Like a spider with a web."

Beretti flicked her eyes up to him. "Exactly."

They sat in silence for a long moment, each absorbing the implication.

The last Dogman wasn't just roaming. It wasn't desperate or wounded or scared.

It was continuing what the others started. And it was

planning.

Ben reached out and traced the triangle with a thick finger, his nail scratching faintly against the paper. "And the center of all this?"

Beretti tapped it lightly. "The woods behind Darrow's place. Maybe a mile east into the deep timber. That's where it's strongest."

Jacobi dropped his hands to his hips, staring down at the map like he could will it to change. "So it brought that Sasquatch into town deliberately. Lured him."

Beretti's jaw shifted slightly, tension running along her shoulders. "Makes sense now. The Dogman couldn't take them head-on out there. But here? In the open? Disoriented and scared?"

Ben's voice was gravel. "Made it look like the Sasquatch was the threat. Got it killed without even lifting a claw."

Beretti leaned back and rubbed her eyes. "Maybe it's time we bait him instead."

Jacobi looked up. "How?"

Beretti pointed at the map, tapping near Mill Creek. "We

set up a distress call. Something wounded sounding. Play it just inside his triangle, right here off Old Mill Creek Road. See if it takes the bait."

Jacobi grinned faintly. "Turn the hunter into the hunted."

Ben nodded slowly. "That could work. He's territorial. He'll want to investigate anything that sounds weak." He hesitated, then looked at Beretti. "That doesn't sound very safe, though."

Beretti met his eyes. "No. But it's our best chance to stop him."

She looked back at the map. "We need to end this. This thing is escalating its attacks, it has no fear of humans."

Ben held her gaze for a moment, then gave a reluctant nod. "Alright. I'll trust you both."

Beretti gave a sharp nod.

Jacobi grabbed the coffee pot and poured what was left into his mug, grimacing at the bitter dregs. "Tomorrow. Perfect."

Ben grabbed his phone and headed down the hallway. "Get some sleep. It's going to be a long damn day."

CHAPTER 23

The morning passed quickly. They picked up the SUV from Beretti's old house, double-checked supplies, and took time to rest where they could. By the late afternoon, they were gathering their gear, their nerves mixed with anticipation.

Beretti stood by the back door, tightening the strap on her tactical vest. Her movements were methodical, each piece of gear checked twice. On the kitchen table behind her, equipment was laid out in organized rows: flashlights, radios, extra magazines, a battered first aid kit.

Jacobi crouched by one of the duffels, packing up the last of the supplies. "You know," he said, "just once, I'd like a mission where we get to use a flamethrower."

Beretti laughed as she loaded her sidearm. "Yeah, that'd be cool. Right up until you set the whole forest on fire."

Jacobi zipped the duffel closed and slung it over his shoulder. "Fine. I'll save it for the parking lot."

Beretti smirked. "That's the spirit. Burn responsibly."

From the kitchen, the smell of roasted meat and onions drifted through the air. Leoni moved between the stove and the counter, ladling stew into heavy bowls. Her voice was firm but kind. "Sit. Eat something before you head out. You will need it."

Beretti stripped off her gloves and sat down without argument. Jacobi dropped into the seat across from her, already reaching for a spoon.

"You sure you don't want to ride shotgun with us?" Jacobi asked, half-teasing.

Leoni gave him a dry look. "No offense, but I like breathing too much."

A short chorus of excited yaps and huffs from Whiskey and Wink erupted as Ben pushed open the front door and stepped inside.

"Give me a few to shower and change," he said, glancing towards the kitchen before heading down the hall and disappearing into the bathroom. A minute later, the faint sound of the shower echoed through the house.

Beretti picked at her stew more than she ate it. Across from her, Jacobi shoveled it down without hesitation. Leoni set a hand briefly on Beretti's shoulder before sitting down herself with a cup of coffee.

After a few minutes, Leoni glanced toward the back door. "Hey, Nicole. Mind giving me a hand with the dogs?"

Beretti stood and set her bowl aside. "Sure."

They slipped out the back, the door thudding gently behind them. The two little stragglers waddled after them into the yard, tails up and noses to the ground.

Leoni chuckled softly. "Truth is, I didn't need help to wrangle these two. I just wanted to check in. Are you okay?"

Beretti watched one of the dogs sniff around a clump of grass, then glanced over. "My mind's a whirlwind right now. Finding out the truth is… a bitter pill to swallow. But I'll learn to live with it. Eventually."

Leoni gave a quiet nod. "Well, just so you know, I'm always here if you want to talk. No matter where you are."

Beretti smiled faintly. "Thanks."

They followed the dogs up the steps and back into the warmth of the house.

Ben returned not long after, hair still wet, clean shirt stretched across his broad frame. He grabbed a bowl, sat heavily, and ate without small talk.

When the meal was finished, they moved in quiet unison. Beretti checked the bait device one last time, making sure the wounded-animal recording was ready to go. Jacobi ran a final test on the radios. Ben loaded the last of the gear into a battered duffel.

As they gathered their things, Leoni looked up from her coffee. "Is Jacobi driving?"

Beretti smirked. "Probably."

Leoni turned to Jacobi with a cheeky smile. "You better watch out for deer, then."

The others laughed while Jacobi walked over and pulled her into a hug. "I'm sorry. I'll try to stay away from the deer."

Leoni grinned. "That's good for the deer. But it doesn't matter to me in the end. It's not my car you will be driving."

They all chuckled.

Outside, the sun was just beginning to slide behind the distant ridges, casting a dull amber light over the rooftops.

After saying goodbye to Leoni, they hauled the gear out to the SUV parked along the curb. It was loaded now with enough firepower to make a small dent in a war.

Jacobi climbed into the driver's seat. Beretti slid into the passenger side while Ben took the back.

Leoni stood on the porch, arms crossed tightly over her chest. She waved them off and said a quiet prayer as the SUV pulled away.

They headed for Old Mill Creek Road, leaving the last of the town behind.

Ahead, the forest grew thicker, and the night waited.

CHAPTER 24

The SUV rolled to a stop, settling into the uneven turnout off Old Mill Creek Road. Jacobi killed the engine and sat for a moment, listening to the cooling metal tick under the hood and the steady, unbroken quiet outside the vehicle.

"I should've had a strong coffee before we left," Jacobi said. "These stakeouts tend to drag on for hours."

Beretti glanced over at him. "Probably best you didn't. You'd be jittery and making too much noise."

Jacobi nodded. "Fair comment."

A tense stillness lay over the woods, more suffocating than the last time they had scouted this spot. The air was unmoving. No insects stirred. Just a quiet that clung to everything and raised goosebumps without reason.

Jacobi adjusted the strap on his vest and leaned forward,

peering through the windshield. "Spooky," he mumbled under his breath. "Let's get this show on the road."

Beretti did not answer. She pushed open the door and stepped out into the cooling evening air. The ground was damp and soft, sucking slightly at her boots. The forest loomed on all sides, the trees black against a sky that was sliding fast into bruised purple.

Ben came around from the back seat, grabbing the bait device out of the back. It looked crude, a cracked speaker zip-tied to a salvaged military-grade battery pack, but it would do the job.

Beretti checked her gear automatically. Sidearm holstered tight against her hip. Rifle slung across her back. Extra magazines clipped to her vest.

A faint breeze stirred the trees, brushing cool across her face. She tasted damp earth and old pine in the air. The wind was blowing toward them, back toward the road. It was in their favor. Their scent would not carry deep into the woods.

"Same plan?" Jacobi asked, voice pitched low.

Beretti nodded. "We go in about a hundred and fifty yards. Set up the bait near that cluster of deadfalls I saw on the satellite map. High ground there gives us sightlines back to the road."

Ben grunted approval, already checking the safety on his shotgun. "Let's move."

CHAPTER 25

They moved into the tree line, boots muffled by thick layers of fallen needles and soft earth. Within ten steps, the SUV was gone behind a wall of trees.

Beretti led, rifle raised. Jacobi watched their six. Ben carried the bait device.

The deeper they went, the more unnatural the stillness became.

They reached the deadfalls. Fallen trunks jutted from the soil like bones, long since bleached and splintered. Beretti signaled them down. Jacobi moved ahead to check the treeline while Ben crouched to set up the device.

Beretti knelt beside him, eyes sweeping the woods. Her rifle felt solid in her grip, her pulse steady.

Ben finished the setup and nodded once.

Beretti gave the quiet go ahead.

The device let out a single chirp, and the rabbit's cry started. High and panicked. A jagged sound that cut through the trees like glass dragged across metal.

They pulled back into the low brush and flattened themselves against the earth.

The sound echoed out again.

And again.

Minutes passed.

At first, nothing stirred. Just the cry looping, unanswered.

A faint crack followed. A twig underfoot. A leaf disturbed. Another soft snap closer, almost rhythmic. Something was moving out there, slow and low.

Beretti stayed still, eyes narrowing.

The rabbit scream looped again.

From the left, a shape crept into view. A coyote. Thin and ragged. Its ribs shifted under the skin. It stepped lightly, sniffing at the air. Head lowered. Ears twitching.

It paused near the bait.

Nostrils flared.

It froze.

Turned hard and sprinted back into the trees, gone in seconds.

Beretti didn't lift her head. Her body stayed locked in position. Her muscles ached from stillness, but she didn't move.

Jacobi let out a slow, tight breath. "Christ," he mumbled. "Thought we had something."

Beretti lowered her rifle slightly but did not relax. "We do. Just not yet."

The coyote had come to investigate the easy meal.

Something smarter, something hungrier, would not announce itself so easily.

Five more minutes. Then ten.

Another snap echoed through the timber. A dry branch breaking under something large. Then something heavier brushed along a tree trunk, dragging just enough to raise every instinct.

The rabbit cry kept screaming. Its pitch grew more unbearable each time it restarted.

A chorus of yipping broke out to the north. Coyotes, abrupt and rising, their calls bouncing off the ridge. Several at once. Some closer, some deeper into the woods.

Snarls and barks followed.

The noise whipped itself into a frenzy.

Jacobi said, without looking, "What the hell?"

Beretti didn't respond.

A half-second later, something growled behind her.

It wasn't just deep.

It thundered through her chest.

A vibration low enough to shake the inside of her bones.

Heat brushed her neck.

She rolled hard, shoulder to dirt, rifle swinging up.

The Dogman was already leaning over her, snarling with

lips peeled back and teeth slick with saliva.

Her rifle cracked.

The bullet clipped the side of its skull, just above the eye.

It hissed and twisted backward, crashing into the underbrush.

Beretti scrambled to her feet.

"Behind us!" she yelled.

Ben spun around, shotgun lifted. Jacobi leapt up, rifle turning with him.

They scanned the treeline, but nothing moved.

A rustle off to the left.

A crack behind them.

The rabbit cry continued, a mechanical scream carving through the quiet.

Jacobi whispered, "It's too fast."

His gaze lifted toward the canopy.

"It's in the trees!" he yelled.

The branches above them swayed gently. Nothing definite. Just enough to suggest movement.

Ben adjusted his grip, breathing hard.

Another brush of movement to the right.

Then silence.

A heartbeat passed.

The Dogman struck.

It launched from the dark and went straight for Ben.

He raised his arm just in time.

Its jaws latched onto his forearm, teeth punching through the fabric of his jacket. He screamed, body twisting as it tried to drag him down.

Beretti aimed, but Ben's body was in the way.

She stepped sideways and fired once.

The round tore into the Dogman's shoulder.

It released Ben with a guttural snarl and leapt away into the trees.

Jacobi fired three times as it vanished into the brush.

The forest snapped quiet.

Ben crumpled to the dirt, clutching his arm. Blood ran through his fingers in thick ribbons.

Beretti was already beside him, rifle in one hand, her other yanking out a compression bandage.

And out in the woods, something waited. Just beyond sight. Just beyond sound. Still watching. Still hungry.

CHAPTER 26

Ben gritted his teeth but dropped to one knee, shotgun still in hand. The color had drained from his face, his jaw clenched so tightly it trembled. Blood ran freely from his forearm where the Dogman had latched on, soaking the fabric dark.

Jacobi stood beside him, rifle sweeping across the trees. "I lost it. Could be circling."

Beretti tied off the compression bandage, fingers slick with blood. "Stay sharp."

Ben's breath hissed through his teeth as he adjusted his grip. "Didn't come for the bait. Came for us."

Beretti gave a single, tight nod.

The bait device wailed on. The sound grated against every nerve.

Jacobi shifted position behind them. "We need to move. Ben's bleeding too much. That trail's going to glow like a beacon."

Beretti slung her rifle and helped Ben to his feet. He staggered once but steadied himself, the shotgun still gripped tight.

They moved together without words. Beretti out front. Ben in the middle. Jacobi at the rear, scanning every flicker of motion.

The trees leaned in closer with every step. Shadows deepened. Branches grew thicker, hanging lower, closing their path into narrow corridors. The ground sucked at their boots, thick with moisture. Loose stones rolled underfoot. Hidden dips waited like traps.

The sound of the bait device finally choked and went quiet behind them.

Now it was just the three of them.

And it.

They walked with caution but not hesitation. Each step carried urgency. Jacobi's boots caught on roots once, and he barely caught himself. Ben stumbled again, breathing like he was forcing each inhale through pain.

Beretti reached back without turning and steadied him.

A snap echoed ahead, dry and hollow.

Jacobi whispered, "Still with us."

They broke through a wall of brush and could see the faint shimmer of moonlight spilling onto the gravel turnout where their SUV waited. It looked impossibly far.

They were maybe forty yards out.

Thirty.

Beretti could already feel her muscles beginning to ease.

A sound lifted in the distance. Not natural. Mechanical. Low and fading, then rising again.

Jacobi's head turned slightly. "You hear that?"

Beretti paused, listening.

The buzzing of engines.

"Four-wheelers," she said. "More than one."

The Dogman had heard it too.

A low shape darted across the treeline ahead, long limbs and heavy gait unmistakable. It was moving fast, cutting away from them.

Beretti's eyes followed its path. She turned.

"It's headed toward the four-wheelers."

Jacobi tensed. "Shit."

Beretti looked at him. "Get him to the SUV. Call for backup. I'm going after it."

Jacobi hesitated. "Beretti…"

"Get him to the car, Jacobi," she snapped. "He needs help. You do not leave him. Not until someone gets here. I've gotta end this."

He looked like he wanted to argue, but one glance at Ben shut it down.

Beretti turned and ran.

The woods tangled around her like a moving net.

Branches whipped her arms. Thorns scraped across her cheek. Roots tugged at her boots. She pushed forward, breath short, and legs driving, her rifle tucked close.

Somewhere ahead, the engines were louder. She heard laughter, rising over the mechanical growl. They had no idea what was coming.

Beretti changed direction without thinking, chasing the sound. Her lungs burned. Her body ached.

She could hear something crashing through the trees. Snapping limbs. Heavy steps.

A scream cracked the night.

She broke through a tangle of brush and hit a narrow trail, her boots sliding slightly on the soft dirt.

Ahead, in the low light of two four-wheelers, a nightmare unfolded.

A young man lay on the ground, chest exposed. Blood soaked through his shirt. The Dogman crouched over him, massive jaws latched onto his ribs, ripping. Flesh tore with a sound like wet cloth. Bone showed under the torn muscle.

A young woman stood off to the side. Screaming. Frozen.

Beretti brought up her rifle.

"Move!" she yelled.

The woman didn't react. Just that awful scream.

Beretti sprinted forward, drove her shoulder into the woman's side, pushing her away from the line of fire. She dropped to one knee and fired.

The round slammed into the Dogman's back.

It arched and snarled, spinning to face her. Yellow teeth glistened wet in the dark. Blood clung to its mouth.

It hesitated.

Beretti chambered another round.

The Dogman hissed, dropped to all fours, and vanished into the trees.

Beretti ran to the young man. His chest was shredded. Holes opened down to the bone. His eyes were wide, filled with pain and confusion. He tried to speak but only blood came out.

"You're alright," she said. "It's okay. I've got you. Help is coming."

He blinked. Lips moved again.

She held pressure on the worst of the wounds, kneeling

in his blood. "You're not alone."

His head tilted slightly. Then stilled.

The scream behind her had stopped.

Beretti looked up.

The young woman stood nearby, face streaked with tears, hands shaking.

Beretti stood slowly.

"Can you ride?"

The woman didn't answer.

Beretti stepped closer. "Look at me. Can you ride?"

The woman blinked rapidly. "Yes. I think... yes."

"Good. Get back on your four-wheeler. Go the way you came. Don't stop. Don't look back. Just ride until you see help."

The woman was still crying, her face streaked with dirt and panic, but she obeyed. She climbed onto the second vehicle with shaking hands and turned it. The engine caught.

Tires spun against the soil and the machine roared forward, disappearing into the trees.

Beretti stayed still, eyes locked on the direction the Dogman had gone.

She lifted her rifle again.

And ran.

CHAPTER 27

The trail narrowed and twisted through thick undergrowth, clawing at her legs and arms. Branches slapped across her face, thorns scraped skin, but she kept her focus forward.

She could feel the Dogman's path, its weight, its urgency. Blood marked its passing in short, dark drops on the leaves and dirt. The forest didn't welcome her now. It resisted every step.

The engine noise behind her faded. She was alone in the dark.

The ground climbed. A rocky ridge loomed ahead, the incline steep but manageable. She dug in her heels and scrambled up, one hand gripping tree roots to steady herself. The air had gone colder. Damp. No wind.

At the top, the path forked.

She paused, caught her breath, and turned left.

A streak of red marked a broken limb, snapped halfway through. Another smear dragged across a stone just ahead. Blood. Still fresh. Still wet.

She was close.

Her boots whispered over the forest floor, each step cautious now. Her eyes moved constantly, tracking broken brush, torn leaves, bent grass. It wasn't running straight. It was moving wild. Wounded. But not weak.

Her foot hit a loose stone.

She adjusted, took one more step…

The hit came from the side.

Blinding.

A blur of weight and claws slammed into her ribs and knocked her sideways through a curtain of undergrowth. Her rifle flew from her grip, lost in the tangle of limbs and wet leaves. She hit the ground hard, the wind punched out of her. Her shoulder flared with pain that shot up into her neck and down through her chest.

She rolled once, gasping.

The pain in her shoulder screamed. Dislocated, maybe. Or just badly wrecked. She couldn't move it right.

Leaves crackled nearby.

She reached across her body, gritting her teeth as she yanked her pistol from its holster. Her thumb found the safety and clicked it off. Her legs kicked hard beneath her as she shoved herself upright and staggered forward, ducking through the brush. She focused on controlling her breathing through the pain, keeping each inhale calm and anchored.

A snarl sounded behind her, deep and wet.

She didn't look.

Beretti fired a single shot over her shoulder, not to kill but to warn, to slow it down.

She kept running.

The trail twisted tighter.

She didn't stop.

CHAPTER 28

Branches clawed at Beretti's face and neck as she pushed through the brush.

She grunted at the sting but kept moving. Turning back wasn't a choice.

The trail ahead was narrow, knotted with roots and broken stone, but it was the only way forward.

The SUV and safety were somewhere beyond it.

She could hear the Dogman behind her now, a low, rattling growl weaving between the trees.

It wasn't running full speed. She'd shot it twice.

At least it was hurting too.

Beretti forced her legs to move faster. Her breath burned her throat raw.

The air grew sharper, colder, the taste of blood and fear clinging to it.

Ahead, the trail twisted through the trees, the moonlight flashing pale across the broken path.

She took a deep breath, trying to concentrate.

She rounded a bend at full speed and caught the massive figure standing in the trail.

She did not slow.

She dove sideways into the undergrowth without thinking, hitting the cold ground hard and rolling onto her side, sidearm already up.

Her sore shoulder exploded with pain, white lights flaring behind her eyes. She shook her head hard, forcing the nausea back, clinging to whatever clarity she had left.

The Dogman tore down the trail behind her, jaws wide and slavering, claws stretched forward.

It never saw the Sasquatch's fist until it was too late.

The blow struck square across the Dogman's muzzle with a sound like a mountain collapsing.

Hundreds of tiny fractures splintered out from the impact point.

The Dogman's snout flattened grotesquely under the raw force.

Skin split open in jagged tears, dark blood spraying sideways as cartilage and bone exploded under the pressure.

The Dogman gave a strangled yelp, a wet, awful sound that gurgled halfway through.

It staggered backward, pawing blindly at what was left of its face.

Blood gushed through its fingers as it tried to hold itself together.

Each breath rattled and gurgled, a broken, wheezing gasp through ruined airways.

The Dogman stumbled and scraped at the dirt, hind legs buckling.

One eye was already swollen shut, the other glassy and wide, filled with shock and raw agony.

The Sasquatch moved without pause.

It seized the Dogman by the legs, lifted it like a rag, and smashed it into the ground with a roar of impact. The ground quivered under Beretti's hands.

The Dogman gave a feeble kick.

The Sasquatch hauled it up again and slammed it down a second time, harder.

The forest floor cracked open beneath the force. Bones snapped with a deep, wet crunch.

The Dogman went limp, legs splaying awkwardly across the dirt.

The Sasquatch straightened over the broken body, chest rising and falling with deep, slow breaths.

It lifted one massive foot and stomped down onto the Dogman's shattered head, a sloppy crunch echoing through the trees.

The Dogman's body twitched once and then lay still, the last breath leaking out of its ruined chest.

Satisfied, the Sasquatch stepped forward and released a long stream of urine across the Dogman's remains.

The final mark of ownership and dominance.

It turned toward Beretti, massive frame hulking against the ragged shafts of moonlight.

A deep huff thundered from its chest, low and rumbling, more a warning than a greeting.

Then it turned and walked into the woods, disappearing without a sound.

Beretti stayed low for a few more seconds, her sidearm loose in her grip, heart hammering inside her chest.

The air reeked of blood, piss, and broken earth.

She forced herself to breathe.

To focus.

To lock every detail into memory.

The trail.

The layout.

The direction the Sasquatch had gone.

When her body stopped trembling, she pushed herself up.

Her shoulder screamed again, pulsing from the earlier dislocation and now scraped raw from the tree branches.

The white flashes were back again, streaking across her vision like sparks from a live wire. She struggled to breathe, chest tight and uneven. The nausea hit hard and deep. Her stomach lurched, and this time she couldn't stop it. She turned her head and vomited into the leaves, the motion sending another jolt of pain through her shoulder. Her vision blurred. She wiped her mouth with the back of her hand and forced herself to move, to crawl forward, to stay alert.

A few minutes later with her breathing under control, Beretti put her gun away, checked her phone for the GPS, and headed down the trail towards Jacobi and Ben.

She did not look back.

CHAPTER 29

Beretti walked slowly along the narrow trail, her boots dragging through the loose soil. Every step sent fresh pain through her shoulder, but she kept going, eyes fixed ahead, one foot in front of the other.

The branches thinned, and a beam of flashlight swept across the trees.

"Nicole?" Jacobi's voice carried out of the dark, sharp with concern.

She looked up. He was already hurrying toward her, rifle slung, with obvious relief.

"I've got you," he said, slipping an arm around her back to steady her. "Come on, let's get you out of here."

She didn't resist. The adrenaline had burned out, and what was left was a deep ache that settled in her bones and throbbed sharply in her injured shoulder.

"Ben?" she asked, her voice soft and rough.

"He's okay," Jacobi said. "They've got the bleeding under control and hit him with some pain relief."

Beretti nodded slowly, her lips pressed into a line. She leaned a little more of her weight into Jacobi as they made their way back down the trail.

"You need help too," he added. "You look like hell."

Beretti gave a short breath through her nose that might have been a laugh.

They moved in silence for a while, the night air cooling the sweat along her spine. Behind them, the trees were still and quiet.

After a few more steps, she said, "The Dogman killed one of the four-wheel riders. Check if the female made it out. She should've come out on Johnson Creek Road."

Jacobi kept his eyes on the trail. "I'll handle it."

Eventually, the faint sound of voices reached them, along with the flicker of emergency lights cutting between trunks.

As they stepped into the clearing, a pair of deputies turned toward them. One rushed forward with a blanket while another flagged over the medic.

Jacobi didn't let go until she was seated, her hand still holding onto his.

CHAPTER 30

The ambulance backed into the emergency bay, jolting slightly as it settled against the curb. The rear doors swung open and paramedics moved quickly, guiding the stretcher down the ramp. Ben lay on it, pale and barely conscious, his arm wrapped in thick bandages where the Dogman had bitten him to the bone.

Beretti sat beside him, her face drawn with pain. Her jacket hung askew, shoulder sagging from the dislocation, arms marked with scrapes and streaks of dirt from the forest floor.

The glass doors parted as two nurses and a trauma doctor met them inside.

"Vitals steady," one paramedic said, moving alongside the stretcher. "Tourniquet applied to the upper arm. Wound is deep, down to the bone. We've given fluids and pain relief."

Ben groaned, too weak to speak.

"He'll need surgery," the doctor said. "Stabilize him tonight. We'll operate in the morning."

They wheeled him off at a brisk pace.

Beretti pushed herself up but swayed, caught by a nurse before she could fall.

"You're next," the nurse said. "Come on."

"I can wait," Beretti mumbled, eyes still fixed on the hallway.

"You can't. That shoulder's out, and you're shaking."

The nurse led her into a small exam room and sat her down.

Another nurse began cutting away the strap of her sling and gently probing the bruised area. Her voice stayed calm.

"Dislocated, looks like. Some abrasions. No major bleeding. We'll get that shoulder back in first."

Beretti nodded once, jaw clenched.

"Ready?"

She grunted in reply.

The nurse gave a short count and with well-trained precision, guided the shoulder back into its socket.

Beretti grunted hard and loud, her breath catching as a wave of pain lit up the back of her eyes. She blinked it away and forced herself to breathe through it.

"Good," the nurse said, taping down a fresh sling. "You'll be sore, but it's back in place."

She cleaned the scrapes and gave Beretti a tetanus shot, then handed over a small cup with four pills and a bottle of water.

"Painkillers. Take two now, and two in the morning."

Beretti swallowed them without comment, eyes still on the hallway.

Jacobi stepped into view a few minutes later. His jacket was zipped up, his face drawn but focused.

"Ben's stable for now," he said. "They're cleaning the wound now and prepping him for surgery in the morning. I see where you get your grit from."

Beretti exhaled, the tension easing just slightly from her

shoulders.

Ten minutes later, Leoni burst through the ER doors. She looked like she had dressed in a hurry, one boot half-zipped and her shirt tucked unevenly into her jeans.

She found Beretti in an instant. "Are you alright?"

Beretti nodded. "Ben's inside. They're treating him now."

Leoni started down the hallway but was intercepted by a nurse before she reached the door.

"They're still working. You can go in soon."

Leoni returned and sat next to Beretti, her hands trembling in her lap.

Jacobi leaned against the wall nearby, arms crossed, saying nothing.

Beretti sat quiet, shoulder braced, body aching. The painkillers were starting to dull the worst of it, but every muscle still throbbed.

Finally, the nurse came back. "You can see him now. One at a time."

Leoni stood and went through the door without a word.

Beretti leaned back against the wall and let her eyes close for a moment. Not to sleep. Just to breathe.

Jacobi stayed close, watchful and quiet.

A few minutes passed before he glanced at his phone, spoke quietly into it, then ended the call and stepped closer.

"The deputies found the female four-wheel rider. She made it out to a nearby residence. Doctor's with her now. Shock, mostly."

Beretti looked over.

Jacobi added, "They'll send a team to recover the male's body tomorrow morning. The Dogman's body will be removed too."

Beretti gave a slight tilt of her head in acknowledgment, then leaned her head back against the wall again, eyes drifting shut.

CHAPTER 31

The house was still when Beretti woke. Thin morning light pushed through the blinds, casting long gray lines across the floor.

She sat up slowly, stiff from the night before.

Her shoulder ached with every small movement.

She pushed back the blanket and swung her legs over the edge of the bed.

She checked her phone noting it was just after 6am. A hush that settled over everything, waiting for the world to move again.

In the kitchen, she ran the tap until it turned cold and splashed water on her face.

The bandage on her arm was already loosening.

Outside, the world was damp.

Rain had passed sometime in the early hours, leaving the porch slick and the air cool.

A single crow perched on the railing.

Its feathers were dark and soaked through, but its eyes were bright.

It watched her without moving.

Beretti paused in the doorway, hand resting on the frame.

She watched it with curiosity.

It stayed for a few seconds, then gave a short, rough call and flew off toward the trees.

She stepped onto the porch and looked at her phone.

The screen lit up with a new message.

Recovered. Loaded and secured. Shipping out by noon.

She stared at the words for a few seconds, then tapped out a reply.

Copy.

The Dogman was gone.

Not just dead, but collected, accounted for, handled. There was a kind of finality to that, though it didn't bring peace.

Just the next step.

They hoped that was the last of them. If it wasn't, then maybe the Sasquatch would take care of it.

She headed back inside just as Jacobi was walking up the hallway, rubbing sleep from his eyes with the back of one hand.

He had thrown on a hoodie and boots, same pants from the night before.

His face was marked with the same tired calm she felt. He smiled and took a seat at the table without speaking.

She held up the phone so he could see the message.

"Dogman's body has been picked up. They're shipping it out today."

Jacobi nodded and leaned back in the chair.

"Good. That's one mess contained."

Beretti sat down beside him.

Eventually Jacobi said, "You sleep at all?"

Beretti looked over at him.

"A little."

"You eat anything?"

"Not yet."

Jacobi stood and moved into the kitchen without another word.

She watched the window while Jacobi put on some coffee.

The crow didn't come back.

But she knew it would.

CHAPTER 32

Under the soft warmth of the afternoon sun, Beretti stepped out onto the back porch, phone in hand, the two dogs trotting down the steps to do their business.

Somewhere in the branches above, a bird called out once and went quiet again.

She sat on the top step, the one with the slight crack near the edge, and scrolled through her contacts until she found Ward's name.

It rang twice before he picked up.

"Beretti," he said.

His voice was alert, but not rushed.

"Morning, sir," she said. "Just giving you a situation update."

"Go ahead."

"The Dogman is confirmed dead. The carcass was recovered at first light and is being transported now. No sign of others. No secondary threats."

There was a short pause on the line.

"You sound tired."

She gave a soft exhale. "Yeah. It was a long one."

"You did good," Ward said, then let her continue.

She hesitated for a moment, then said, "There's something else."

"Go on."

She shifted slightly, looking out toward the edge of the woods.

Her voice stayed steady, but lower now.

"I found out what really happened to my parents. I didn't expect it. None of this was even part of the original file. But it came up during the investigation. A Sasquatch was involved. Not a random one either. One of the older ones, a known problem. Locals had stories going back years."

Ward didn't interrupt.

She appreciated that.

"For about a day after I found out," she said, "I disappeared. I left. Didn't check in. Didn't answer calls. I needed space, and I took it. I know that's not how we're supposed to handle it, but I couldn't be around anyone."

Ward was quiet for a few seconds.

Then he said, "That's more honest than most agents ever are."

"Still shouldn't have let it happen."

"Maybe not," he said. "But I've seen agents go off the rails for less. You came back. You handled the threat. You're not a machine, Beretti. You're human. And what you found out would've cracked anyone."

She let the words sit there.

Not to be comforted, but because they were true.

"Thank you," she said.

"You don't owe me that," he replied. "But I'm glad you told me."

Another pause. Then his tone shifted, lighter.

"You and Jacobi haven't had any time off in over six months."

"Not really," she said.

"Then take it now. Stay in Blackridge for the holidays. Both of you. Rest. Recharge. I'll keep anything new off your plate for the next few weeks."

Beretti looked out toward the trees and the distant ridge beyond them.

For once, staying still didn't feel like failure.

It felt earned.

"I appreciate that," she said.

"We'll stay awhile. It will give us a chance to ensure all Dogmen have been eliminated."

"Good," Ward said. "Take care of yourself, Beretti."

"You too, sir."

She ended the call and sat there for a long moment, letting the quiet settle back in.

Leaves stirred on the ground nearby.

The breeze shifted.

When she finally stood, it was without the drag that had gripped her since yesterday.

Not gone. But manageable.

CHAPTER 33

A light rain had started falling by the time Jacobi pulled in with Ben and Leoni, the driveway slick with fresh puddles.

The truck doors swung open slowly.

Ben moved stiffly but under his own power, wrapped in fresh bandages that ran under his jacket.

His face was ashy but there was a spark in him again, stubborn as ever.

Leoni hovered close but let him walk, only stepping in when he stumbled once near the porch steps.

Beretti was already waiting at the door, a clean towel slung over one shoulder.

The house smelled of meat and herbs, warmth thick in

the air.

"Welcome back," she said simply, stepping aside so they could come in.

Ben grunted as he crossed the threshold, keeping an eye out to not to trip over the excited dogs.

He dropped onto the nearest chair with a slow exhale, Leoni sitting beside him.

Jacobi followed them in, shrugging out of his jacket, the same easy stride even after everything they had been through.

Beretti asked Jacobi to pull the dish from the oven and set it on the table.

The stew simmered thick and fragrant, its rich aroma filling the kitchen.

"Sit," she said to Jacobi, handing him a plate.

"You too," she said to Leoni.

"It was the best I could do with one functional arm," she added.

None of them argued.

They ate quietly for a few minutes, the scrape of spoons and the low hum of the heater filling the space.

Ben pushed back from the table after his second helping and wiped his mouth with a paper napkin.

He looked at Beretti across the table, gaze full of quiet pride.

"You know, kiddo," he said, voice rough with old emotion, "I always knew you were good at this job. But what you pulled off out there... that's another level entirely."

Beretti smiled as she replied. "Just doing the job".

Jacobi leaned back in his chair, nodding in quiet agreement.

Ben glanced at him too.

"You both did good. Better than good. You kept your heads when a lot of people would have lost theirs. You've both got great instincts."

Jacobi lifted his glass slightly.

"Means a lot, Ben. Thank you."

Beretti added, "And thank you both for letting us stay

here. You didn't have to."

"Here, here," Jacobi added.

Leoni waved a hand like it was nothing, but her smile was real.

"You're family," she said simply.

Ben tapped his fingers lightly against the edge of his plate, thoughtful.

He looked at Beretti and Jacobi, then back at his hands.

"Why don't the two of you stay here for the holidays?" he asked.

"It would do you good."

Beretti smiled a little wider.

"Funny you should say that," she said.

"I spoke to ASAC Ward this afternoon. He's giving us the holidays off."

She glanced at Jacobi as she spoke.

Jacobi caught the look and grinned.

Beretti leaned an elbow on the table, looking at him directly. "You want to stay with us?"

Jacobi scooped another piece of beef with his spoon.

"If I keep getting fed like this, hell yeah."

One of the dogs, curled up near the hearth, gave a happy bark as if seconding the decision.

The sound drew a quiet chuckle from the table.

Outside, the rain started to fall, soft against the windows.

Inside, for the first time in a while, there was a semblance of peace.

CHAPTER 34

The road narrowed as they drove, winding deeper into forest that grew darker with every turn. Branches reached overhead like interlocked fingers, and the canopy filtered the afternoon light into shifting patterns across the dashboard.

Beretti had been quiet for most of the drive. One hand on the wheel, the other resting on her lap. Her posture was relaxed, but her expression stayed sharp, focused on the curves ahead.

Jacobi sat in the passenger seat, watching her more than the scenery. He wasn't sure where they were headed exactly, only that it wasn't on any itinerary. But there was something intentional in the way she drove. She hadn't said much, and he knew better than to press it.

Still, he couldn't deny a faint pulse of anticipation in his chest. Not nerves exactly, but something close. He had seen Beretti in plenty of situations: intense, chaotic, dangerous. But this felt different. Calmer. More personal.

"Alright, I can't help it. Are you going to tell me where we're going?" he asked eventually, keeping his tone light.

Beretti's eyes stayed on the road.

"Somewhere special," she said. "It's been a long time coming."

A few turns later, they passed a small wooden sign. It leaned slightly, paint faded, but the words were still clear: **Salmon River**.

Jacobi straightened slightly in his seat.

"Out here? What is this place to you?"

Beretti exhaled slowly, not answering right away. "My mother and grandmother were part of the Karuk tribe," she said. "We don't have a traditional reservation, but the tribe has places along the Salmon where they hold ceremonies. This is one of them. I haven't been back in many years."

He gave a slow nod, his earlier curiosity deepening.

"This should be interesting."

"It will be," she said. "It wasn't something I let myself lean into for a long time. But things change."

A few more minutes passed before the trees began to thin. Ahead, a wide clearing opened near the bend of the river. Several vehicles were parked in a loose row beneath the shade. They pulled in quietly and parked behind a dusty SUV.

Beretti cut the engine and opened the door. Before they had a chance to step out fully, a woman with a long black braid emerged from a small group standing near the water's edge. She moved with grounded confidence, her face brightening the second she spotted Beretti.

"Mara," Beretti said softly.

They met halfway, embracing in a firm, steady hug. "You took your time," Mara said with a smile.

"I know," Beretti replied. "But I'm here now."

Jacobi stepped around the SUV and offered a smile. "Good to see you again, Mara. Glad we're meeting under better circumstances this time."

She laughed lightly.

"We've all had some growing to do. I'm glad we settled our differences."

Beretti looked at her cousin, her expression unreadable for a moment before softening.

"Me too."

They walked down toward the river, where a few others stood waiting. A fire pit had been prepared, low smoke curling upward. Cedar branches hung nearby, and the scent of sage lingered faintly in the air.

Mara motioned toward the gathering.

"The ceremony is about to begin. Cleansing. Grounding. You're taking part?"

Beretti nodded.

"I am."

Mara turned to Jacobi.

"You're welcome to join if you'd like."

He glanced at Beretti, then back to Mara.

"Lay it on me."

They removed their shoes and stepped quietly onto the stones near the fire. Someone handed Beretti and Jacobi a small bundle of herbs wrapped in cloth. They both accepted them silently, holding them in both hands as they listened.

An elder began to speak in a low voice, a mixture of English and Karuk flowing together. The words were soft but carried strength. The river moved steadily beside them, its sound woven into the stillness.

When it was time, Beretti stepped forward. She placed her bundle into the fire without speaking, watching the flames curl around it until the cloth blackened and the smoke rose.

Jacobi followed. He didn't say anything either. Just placed the bundle in the fire and then returned to her side.

The ceremony ended quietly. No applause. No announcement. Just a calm that settled over the river and the people standing beside it.

They turned back toward the others. Mara stepped forward, joined by several familiar faces, some Beretti hadn't seen since childhood.

"It's good to have you back," one of the women said.

"You were missed," another added.

Beretti nodded, voice low.

"It means a lot."

Mara gave her a warm smile.

"You're always welcome here."

Beretti looked from her cousin to the others, then out across the river.

A crow watched her from a low branch, head tilted slightly. It let out a single sharp call before lifting off and disappearing into the canopy.

She felt relieved.

Mara rested a hand gently on Beretti's arm.

"We're heading back to the house soon. Come eat with us. We're putting together a proper lunch."

Beretti glanced at Jacobi, who gave a small shrug and a smile.

"Sounds perfect," he said.

Beretti looked back at Mara.

"We'd love to."

CHAPTER 35

The town of Blackridge had settled into a strange stillness.

A week had passed since the last Dogman was killed. There'd been no fresh sightings, no missing persons, no mutilated livestock. The locals were cautious but relieved, and their caution lingered in the way people locked their doors at sunset and avoided the woods even on clear afternoons.

Beretti sat at the diner with Jacobi and Leoni, the three of them squeezed into a corner booth that smelled faintly of syrup and old coffee. Ben had already left earlier that morning, but not before handing a folder to Beretti thick enough to choke a printer.

They'd finished breakfast not long ago. Eggs, toast and strong coffee that filled and satisfied their bellies.

Jacobi sipped his coffee. "So. This what normal feels like?"

Beretti didn't answer at first. She stirred her tea, eyes on the window. The view overlooked Main Street, where a few locals walked dogs or picked up groceries. Life creeping back in.

"It doesn't feel real," she said. "Like we're all pretending nothing happened."

Leoni reached across the table and gave her hand a squeeze. "People pretend when they don't know what else to do. It's easier than facing what they can't explain."

Beretti nodded slowly. "They'll be alright. They just need time."

Jacobi leaned back. "We all do."

The conversation faded, replaced by the clatter of plates and the hum of a radio in the kitchen. For a while, they sat in companionable silence.

Eventually, Jacobi checked his watch. "We still on for heading back tomorrow?"

Beretti gave a small shrug. "I think I might stay a little longer."

Jacobi raised an eyebrow. "You sure?"

She nodded, glancing toward the window again. "There's just one more thing I want to follow up on."

Leoni tilted her head. "What's that?"

Beretti didn't look at her. She reached down, unzipped her bag, and pulled out a folder tucked beneath her case files. She slid it across the table toward Jacobi.

He picked it up and glanced inside. A stack of printed incident reports. Dates. Locations. Descriptions.

"Local sightings," he said. "From the past five years."

Beretti nodded. "I've got older ones too. Some dating back decades. But those are the most recent. Every one of them describes the same thing. Red eyes. Aggressive behavior. Same area. Same pattern."

Jacobi's eyes met hers. "You're going after him."

Beretti didn't answer, but she didn't deny it either.

She stood, finished the last of her tea, and tucked the folder back into her bag.

"There's still one score I need to settle here," she said

quietly.

Jacobi stood too, watching her. "You sure that's the road you want to walk?"

Beretti adjusted her coat. "I don't think I've got a choice."

Leoni looked between them but said nothing. She just gave Beretti a long, thoughtful look, then nodded once like she understood something neither of them had said aloud.

Beretti stepped out onto the sidewalk, the early light soft against the pavement. A breeze tugged at her hair. The forested hills in the distance were still and green, but she didn't trust that quiet. Not yet.

Jacobi fell in beside her, matching her stride as they walked toward their SUV. He didn't ask what came next.

He already knew.

ABOUT THE AUTHOR

 Luka T. Jacobs, an author from the picturesque Illawarra region south of Sydney, Australia, is passionate about cryptids like Sasquatch and Dogman. She lives there with her partner and their dog, Finnigan.

Luka's love for animals and adventure fuels her storytelling. With a background in Graphic Design and Art, she adds a unique visual flair to her work. An avid traveler and explorer, she draws inspiration from the wild, eager to share her imaginative worlds with readers.

Luka T. Jacobs

Stay connected and join the conversation! *Follow me on Facebook to interact and share your thoughts, explore my books on Amazon, and visit my website for more information about my works and upcoming releases. Don't forget to sign up for my newsletter, you'll be the first to hear about new books, exclusive content and special offers!*

FB: https://www.facebook.com/lukatjacobs
A: https://amazon.com/author/lukatjacobs
W: http://www.LukaTJacobs.com

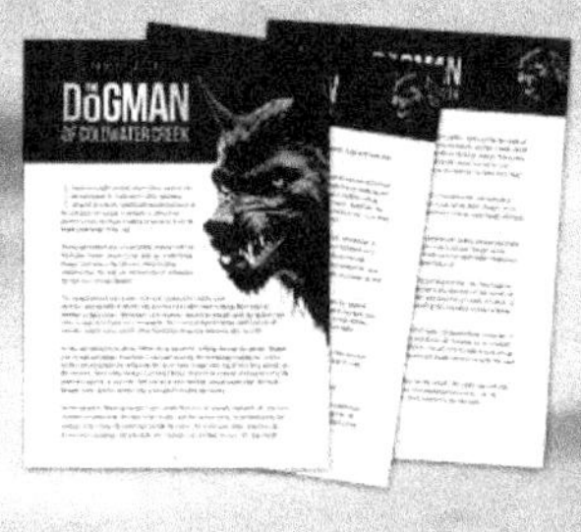

JOIN CRYPTID HORROR CENTRAL

Join my email list and get first access to new releases and download my **FREE** short story *"The Dogman of Coldwater Creek"*.

WWW.LUKATJACOBS.COM

Dear Reader,

Thank you for diving into my book amidst a sea of choices, it truly means the world to me.

If you enjoyed the story, I'd love it if you shared your experience with others and left a review. As an independent author, your voice helps bring these tales to life for more readers, and every recommendation makes a tremendous impact.

Thank you again for joining me on this journey.
I'm so grateful to have you as a reader!

SNEEK PEEK:
FOREST OF THE
SASQUATCH: THEIR
TERRITORY, THEIR RULES

The forest breathed its ancient rhythm. High above, the towering pines swayed in the fall breeze, their needles whispering secrets carried through ancient shadows. Sunlight filtered through the dense canopy, dappling the forest floor in patches of amber and gold.

Hidden deep within the Superior National Forest, near Devil's Track Lake, where the trees cast the deepest shadows, lay a place untouched by humans, the clan's secret sanctuary.

Even the animals of the forest seemed to sense the boundary of this sacred ground, avoiding it entirely. Deer grazed near its edges but never crossed into its heart. Birds flew above the cliffs but rarely landed near the cave's entrance. The natural world seemed to understand what the hairless ones could not: this place belonged to the Sasquatch alone.

Thick, unyielding walls of thorny thicket and dense

brush surrounded the area, growing so tightly together that even the smallest creatures struggled to pass through. Towering trees formed a natural barrier, their twisted roots and low-hanging branches weaving into an almost impenetrable maze. Beyond the thicket, a sheer cliff face rose abruptly from the earth, its jagged surface streaked with moss and lichen. At its base, hidden among boulders and shadows, was the entrance to a vast cave system, cool and damp, where the clan had lived for generations.

The caves were a place of safety, a haven where the family slept, gathered, and raised their young. Here, in this untouched wilderness, the Sasquatch thrived, living in harmony with the forest. But their peace was fragile. The hairless ones had grown bold, venturing deeper into the forest, leaving trails of destruction in their wake.

Aluk crouched low beneath the brush, his eyes glinting as he watched a pair of hairless ones far below. He and his brother Matto had left the sanctuary to patrol the edges of their territory, as they often did when the hairless ones grew too bold. What they saw now made Aluk's fists clench.

The two hairless ones had arrived in a roaring metal beast, its tires gouging deep ruts into the soft earth. They had parked it at the edge of a clearing, its bulk looming like an unwelcome guest. One of them, a tall hairless one in a bright orange jacket, was crouched over the lifeless body of a deer, its glossy eyes staring blankly into the dirt. The hairless one's hands were red with blood as he hacked at the carcass with a hunting knife, his movements rough and careless.

The second hairless one, stocky with a scruffy beard, stood nearby, gathering sticks. "Told you this spot was good," he said, his voice carrying across the clearing. "Nobody comes out this far."

"Think they'll notice one less deer?" the tall hairless one asked, his laugh sharp and grating.

Aluk growled softly, his breath steaming in the cool evening air. His eyes darted to the thunder stick lying in the dirt near the stocky one's feet. A weapon capable of death from a distance, one the clan had learned to fear.

The deer was theirs. The clan depended on these woods for food. The hairless ones had not only invaded their sacred ground, they had stolen from it.

Matto placed a hand on Aluk's shoulder, his claws brushing against the coarse hair there. Through gestures and images, Matto conveyed his thoughts: *Hold. Wait. The Elder forbids this.*

Aluk's response came in a flood of sharp, vivid images: the

hairless ones' bloody hands, their trash scattering across the sacred ground, the machine scarring the earth. *They destroy. They take. How much longer will we watch?*

Matto hesitated. He shared Aluk's anger, but the Elder's warning rang in his mind. The Elder had long insisted on secrecy, on patience. But patience had not stopped the hairless ones from encroaching farther each year.

Hidden in the tree line, Aluk, and Matto crouched, watching as the hairless ones built their red-breath. The breath licked high into the sky, casting flickering shadows on the trees. One of the hairless ones stood and stretched, letting out a loud belch.

"I'm gonna take a piss," he said, stumbling toward the forest's edge.

The men wrinkled their noses as an awful stench wafted toward them. It was rank and overpowering, like garbage left out in the sun for days, layered with a heavy musk that clung to the back of their throats.

"Geez, what is that smell?" one of them mumbled, turning his head away.

Aluk's massive body tensed. He glanced at Matto, who raised a hand in warning. The elder's unspoken message was clear: *hold back. Watch, but do not act.*

But Aluk's mind surged with defiance. He sent an image of the hairless ones laughing, their red-breath consuming the sacred ground, the machine scarring the earth. *Enough.*

As the hairless one staggered toward the trees, Aluk shifted silently from his vantage point, slipping through the thick underbrush. His movements were precise, his hulking frame ghostlike in the moonlight as he circled closer. The rustle of the leaves, the crack of twigs, sounds that would have betrayed a human, blended seamlessly with the forest's natural rhythm.

The hairless one stopped a few feet from the tree line, fumbling with his belt. Aluk waited, crouched just beyond the brush, his eyes locked on his target.

Before Matto could stop him, Aluk lunged forward.

The hairless one barely had time to gasp before Aluk's hand clamped over his face, silencing him. In one swift motion, Aluk dragged the hairless one into the thickets. There was a muffled cry, then silence.

Back at the red-breath, the second hairless one looked up, frowning. "Derek?" he called, squinting into the darkness. "Quit screwing around, man."

He heard a faint rustling from the direction Derek had gone. Then, the snapping of branches. A silhouette moved at the edge of the firelight, massive and looming, too large to be anything human.

A wave of panic washed over him, accompanied by a deep, unsettling fear. He stumbled back toward the clearing, nearly tripping over his own feet. His eyes darted around, trying to pierce the blackness. "Derek?" he called again, his voice trembling now.

When no response came, he turned and sprinted toward his four-wheeler parked near the fire. His hands fumbled as he started the machine, the engine roaring to life. The noise echoed through the forest, jarring and unnatural.

"Not sticking around for this crap," he mumbled, his voice shaking as he gripped the handlebars and gunned the throttle. The four-wheeler lurched forward, kicking up dirt and leaves as it sped down the narrow trail towards the clearing's edge.

The trail was dark, lit only by the pale beams of the machine's headlight. The hairless one's pulse quickened, the trees seeming to converge, their shadows alive with an unseen, unsettling presence. He glanced over his shoulder, expecting to see something chasing him.

As he glanced back at the trail, his eyes widened in disbelief.

Standing in the middle of the path was a towering figure, its hair gleaming faintly in the four-wheeler's headlights. The creature's glowing eyes locked on him, and its massive form blocked the trail entirely.

"Jesus Christ!" the hairless one screamed, shifting his weight as he jerked the handlebars in a frantic attempt to avoid the creature.

The four-wheeler skidded out of control, its tires losing traction on the dirt. The hairless one's panic made him overcompensate, and the machine careened off the trail. It slammed headfirst into a tree with a sickening crunch, the force throwing the hairless one forward.

His body hit the tree with brutal force, a sharp thud reverberating in the woods. He crumpled to the ground at its base, groaning in pain. Blood poured from a deep gash on his forehead as he tried to crawl away, but his body betrayed him, too stunned to respond.

Aluk and Matto emerged silently from the darkness.

The brothers towered over the injured hairless one and the machine that had defiled their sacred forest. Aluk's lips curled back in a snarl as he sent an image to Matto: the machine broken, destroyed, its noise silenced forever.

Matto stepped forward first, his massive hands gripping the four-wheeler. With a guttural roar, he lifted the machine as though it weighed nothing and slammed it into the ground. Metal crumpled and shattered under the force.

The hairless one whimpered, struggling to drag himself away. His effort was futile.

Aluk advanced, his eyes cold. His massive hand reached down, cutting off the hairless one's final, strangled scream.

When the forest fell silent once more, the brothers walked back toward the clearing.

The red-breath still burned faintly, casting flickering light across the remains of the deer carcass the hairless ones had stolen from the woods. Aluk crouched beside it, running his massive hands over the animal's body. Its spirit belonged to the forest, not to the hairless ones who had taken it without care or honor.

With a series of deliberate gestures and vivid shared images, Aluk and Matto came to an agreement: the deer would not be left here to rot. Nor would the bodies of the hairless ones remain to poison the sacred ground.

Matto hoisted the deer across his shoulder with ease, its lifeless form dangling against his broad back. His gaze lingered on the thunder stick lying in the dirt, its metal surface gleaming faintly. With a deliberate motion, he bent down, picked it up, and secured it alongside the deer. He had no idea what he was going to do with the weapon, but he knew he couldn't leave it behind for other hairless ones to find and use.

Aluk carried the bodies of the two hairless ones, their weight inconsequential against his immense strength. The brothers cast a final glance at the campsite and disappeared into the forest.

****

As the first light of dawn painted the horizon, the brothers returned to the sanctuary. Matto laid the deer at the center of the main cave, where it would be divided among the clan. Aluk turned to face the Elder, his chest heaving with the weight of his anger and pride.

The Elder's amber eyes flicked from the bloodied brothers to the deer and back again. Aluk's shared images depicted the events: the hairless ones stealing what was not theirs, the loud machine ravaging the land, and the brothers' swift retribution.

The Elder's expression remained unreadable, but his thoughts were firm. *You have acted without permission. You risked exposure.*

Aluk's response came quickly, sharp, and unrelenting: We protected the forest. The hairless ones are no longer. The deer is ours again.

Matto added his agreement, showing an image of the clan gathered around the deer, nourished by what had been stolen. *This is our duty. To guard. To provide.*

The Elder stared at them for a long moment before turning toward the depths of the cave. His final thought was projected to the whole clan: *You have risked more than you know. But tonight, the forest has been restored.*